TIMELESS GODDESS

Novels By Bernard Cenney:

Sparrow's Tears

Close Your Eyes And See

Timeless Terror

Timeless Soldier

Timeless Embrace

Timeless Destiny

Timeless Paradox

Timeless Goddess

TIMELESS GODDESS
BERNARD CENNEY

Author's Note:

This literary manuscript is entirely a work of fiction. Any similarity or resemblance to businesses, organizations, places, names, characters, real persons, incidents, or events is purely coincidental, unintentional, imaginary, or used in a fictitious manner.

In Memoriam:

JAMES B. CENNEY
19 OCT 1989 — 11 OCT 2004

Loved Forever

Send your tax deductible contributions to find a cure for children's hypertrophic cardiomyopathy to:

www.childrenscardiomyopathy.org

Thank you.
Bernard Cenney

Dedication:

Special thanks go to my wife, Kongsri Cenney.

Over thirty-nine years ago in Southeast Asia, Kongsri left her family, her country, and everything that was familiar to her in order to marry a young American Special Forces Captain. She took my hand and never looked back. We have supported each other in conflict and peace, hardship and success, sorrow and joy. Through it all she has loved me unconditionally and never left my side.

Bernard Cenney
Lt. Colonel (Retired)
United States Army

PREFACE

The worst experience to suffer is the death of your child.

The hypertrophic cardiomyopathy death of my fourteen-year-old son, James Cenney, was a tragedy that nothing in this present world can ever make right. James was young, innocent, and just starting life. One day he was playing his guitar; the next day he was not. One day he was playing football and exercising; the next day he was not. One day he was going to school, laughing, and joking; the next day he was not. One day he was here — the next day he was gone. No father should outlive his child.

James's unexpected death shattered my wife, my daughters, and me. Parents who lose their child never bounce back. Speaking for myself, his death eroded my spirit, my resiliency, my resolve, my fortitude, my joy, my hope, and my self-worth. It became impossible to feel any sort of happiness for years.

The sheer madness and incomprehensible horror of his death destroyed my understanding of a loving God. Suffering became a daily companion. I convulsed at the clichés of "all things happen for a reason," or "God never gives us any burden we can't handle." I avoided those who declared they were "blessed by God." It made me feel as if my life was surely cursed by him.

I had seen death before, privately and in my military career. But this was intensely more personal, more visceral, more agonizing. Surely God did not want this to happen; surely God was mourning just as we were; surely God was in despair over this tragedy; surely God — as my father — empathized.

I started to have vivid dreams and visions of James. I documented and kept a record of them all. I could never (and still can't) control the mental image of my son James passing away. I have always (and still do) blame myself for not being able to somehow save him. It became an unimaginable situation. It began replaying itself, over and over, every day of my life. I was in a very dark place.

The military community at Fort Sam Houston provided us with overwhelming support. Group and individual therapy was helpful at first, but soon was not enough for me. Depression developed into apathy to even want to wake up. A terrible schism evolved between wishing for nonexistence, and a father's obligations to the rest of his family.

I just couldn't believe that James had passed away. Sometimes I think he will walk through the door, and everything will be as it once was. After he died, I thought the world would end. In my mind, I waited for the end to come. But it didn't. People went to work, children went to school, and life kept grinding on. My mind tore to pieces over whether to stop moving or to keep pushing onward.

My wife and daughters were suffering terribly as well, perhaps even more than me. Together as a family, we comforted and supported each other. I don't believe it would have been possible for me to move on without the love of my family. I felt that I had to show strength for them. I had to be the father to push everyone onward and hold the family together. If I gave up, I would have failed everyone. I knew that I had to control my grief and move forever onward. These were the thoughts constantly pounding through my mind.

James's death started me to think deeply, perhaps for the first time in my life, and to read incessantly. I read *The Upanishads*, *The Tibetan Book of the Dead*, and *The Bible*. I studied the Greek historians and philosophers: Aeschylus, Aristotle, Epictetus, Herodotus, Plato, and Sophocles. I read works by Billy Graham, Dalai Lama, Deepak Chopra, Dr. Melvin Morse, and Dr. Raymond Moody, to name just a few. I devoured just about any book that dealt with the subject of reincarnation and life after death. *The New Testament* was the enlightened example to me that life is suffering, and you must force yourself through the pain and move forward.

Pain and suffering must be understood and fully absorbed. You cannot deaden the feelings. You cannot even attempt to understand life without suffering. The message I gleaned from *The Gospel of John* brought hope to me. Sometimes a spiritual transcendence can occur from experiencing intense sorrow.

What I understood for myself was disconcerting. Tragedy strikes everyone. Those who think they are immune, only have but to wait. It will come. More tragedy is lingering around the corner. Life is the great equalizer. You cannot barter for a better life. You must push on through tragedy with all the strength you have inside. Despite unanswered prayers, you must forever move forward and do what's right. To be alive is to have constant pain and struggle.

You must push yourself forward. You must pray. You must master discipline. You must keep focus. You must practice compassion. You must hone understanding. You must think. Learn to speak less, and listen more. Put others first and yourself second. Try to help as many people as you can in your life, and if you can't help them at least don't hurt them. The best possible life you can have is one of helping others, and constantly striving to do what is right, regardless of the outcome.

How do you know what is right? Search your heart. Buddha is about compassion; Jesus is about love. Put those together and it's pretty powerful. Treat everyone with dignity, respect, love, and compassion. The reward you receive is the knowledge and peace of mind that you did what was right.

I spent a career in the US Army continually taking and giving orders, and telling soldiers what to do. I came to an understanding that I could not control events. All I could do was try to lead a good life, help others, and set a positive example. I have failed over and over again. My joy comes from helping others when I can, and watching my children excel and lead good lives.

Now to the subject of my novels.

Writing the books *Sparrow's Tears, Close Your Eyes and See, Timeless Terror, Timeless Soldier, Timeless Embrace, Timeless Destiny, Timeless Paradox,* and *Timeless Goddess* became therapy for me — the best therapy. When I think of my son James, I see him always helping others — those who could not help themselves — whether at home or in school. He made me realize that nothing is without purpose; that there is a majestic plan which unfolds itself across the vastness of time equally embracing each life, no more or less important than another. Writing the novels became my way of honoring and paying tribute to James. It allowed me to envision him as an adult, giving him the type of life I would have wished for him. Writing the books allowed me to dream my son a life which I felt had ended too quickly. James Cenney is alive in the pages of my novels. He encourages my readers and me to move forever forward in life.

The hero of my novels — Captain James Ross — is patterned after my son. They both have the same looks, style, loves, and ambience. They are both heroes. But even more than that, as my son James Cenney would say, they "… are intelligent human beings."

My fervent hope is that anyone who is suffering from PTSD and depression can use fiction writing as therapy.

Bernard Cenney
Floresville, Texas

TIMELESS GODDESS

PART ONE

How you are fallen from Heaven, O Lucifer, son of the morning! How you are cut down to the ground, you who laid the nations to waste!

Isaiah 14:12

PROLOGUE

WOLF'S LAIR 1944

Der Führer was growing impatient with his staff.

Why couldn't they understand? Is this the limit of their capacity? Why do I have to constantly explain everything over and over?

Adolf Hitler, the Führer and Reichskanzler (Leader and Chancellor of the Reich) was receiving a briefing from his High Command staff officers at the Wolf's Lair.   Located in the Masurian woods near Rastenburg in Poland, the Wolf's Lair got its name from the self-adopted nickname of Hitler himself. It was constructed to allow Hitler a forward command post to direct Operation Barbarossa, which was the codename for the Nazi invasion of the Soviet Union. There was a series of buildings which included communications posts, barracks, headquarters, and two-meter-thick (six-feet-seven-inch) steel reinforced concrete bunkers surrounded and protected by anti-aircraft guns, Panzer tanks, two thousand of Heinrich Himmler's crack SS (Schutzstaffel) troopers, and acres of landmines.

Hitler was seated at the head of a ten foot, highly polished, rectangular oak table. Surrounding him were his generals — Keitel, Schmitt, Blomberg, Rommel, Jodl, and Kammler. Reichsminister of Aviation Hermann Göring sat directly opposite to Hitler. Göring was rotund, flamboyant, and always flaunting his Blue Max medal at the others. The Reichführer of the Schutzstaffel, Heinrich Himmler, sat on Göring's left. Himmler was a diminutive man with a tiny moustache, pale skin, and ever-present small circular glasses behind which concealed his lifeless blue eyes and debauched sadomasochism. To Himmler's left sat the youthful Albert Speer, the Minister of Armaments and War Production.

Hitler looked across the table and said, "What do you think Speer?"

Thirty-nine-year-old Albert Speer measured his words very carefully. "My Führer, I believe we can win the war with these marvelous new and exciting weapons. Von Braun's V-1 and V-2 rockets shall continue to pummel England and bring her to her knees. Our jet engineered Messerschmitt Me 262s will continue their aeronautical advantage over the enemies obsolete fighters, and I believe Die Glocke is now operationally ready."

Speer confidently looked across the table at General Kammler for support.

Obergruppenführer Hans Friedrich Kammler served the Third Reich with distinction. As a member of the Schutzstaffel or SS, Kammler managed engineer requirements, and was in charge of the Special Projects Division for the Führer. Special Projects included the Führer's wonder-weapons. These wunderwaffe were Hitler's gift to the future. Kammler oversaw everything, from the revolutionary Horten 229 jet flying wing aircraft to the breathtaking V-2 missile attack systems. Hans Kammler was one of the esteemed Councilors of the Interior. He was personally in command of the Die Glocke project, which was codenamed Operation Chronos.

General Hans Kammler quickly replied, "My Führer, Operation Chronos is complete. Our physicists have finished putting Die Glocke prototypes through their final test runs. Full-scale production has begun. We already have three machines primed."

Hitler thought for a second. *Everything happens in time.*

The Greek word for 'time' is *chronos.*

Chronos was considered a God in pre-Socratic Greek philosophy, and was the son of Uranus — God of the sky. Chronos wounded his father, and from the blood was born the Furies — female spirits of vengeance and justice.

The Nazis were obsessed with Teutonic and Norse myths.

In Norse mythology, the world was depicted as a tree — the tree of the world — known as Yggdrasil. Odin's Kingdom of the Nine Realms was attached to Yggdrasil. Chronos has been depicted as a serpent wrapped around Yggdrasil. The world will come to an end when the serpent lets go of Yggdrasil, or so it was believed in ancient times.

Operation Chronos was the codename for Nazi Germany's secret attempt to master space-time vortex compression.

The Third Reich was using German Professor Albert Einstein's special and general relativity laws of physics for gravity as a curvature of space-time, and the relationship of time to gravity absence.

The experiments utilized thorium-nitrate emulsion, beryllium-peroxide fusion, xerum-methane separation, and mercury displacement. Nazi scientists had produced the desired magnetic field separation outcomes at high intensity counter-rotating speeds. Nazi physicists and mechanical engineers had solved the issue of antigravity time dilation. The Henge test site was used for the antigravity propulsion trials. Success had been achieved.

The resulting manufactured device was about the size and weight of a sedan standing on end, only more so resembling a very large bell. Hence, its German nickname became *Die Glocke,* or in English simply *the Bell.* All this had been accomplished at the Riese facility near the Czechoslovakian border.

On the surface, Hitler indulged in Himmler's Aryan and Teutonic superiority myths. But deep inside he was a ruthless politician and a soldier. He was a realist. Hitler believed in what he could see and conquer with brute force. But, if believing in esoteric magic led to victory, then so be it.

Chronos could be proved theoretically on the chalk board, but had the capacity to enter the realm of something mystical — something magical. It was as if science and magic had blended together.

Time won't matter anymore, thought Hitler. *I will own time. I will bring the past and present together. Operation Chronos will bring total victory to my Third Reich.*

The Führer opened a 'Top Secret' labeled folder in front of him and pulled out a photograph of the machine.

The Die Glocke device was approximately nine feet wide and twelve feet tall. It was constructed from a combination of beryllium, magnesium, titanium, and aluminum alloys.   It looked heavy, and weighed approximately four thousand pounds.   Its color was a faded dark metallic gray.   Electronic cables crisscrossed around its base and up to its top.   There was a hatch with a nautical locking wheel on the front of it.   Circling around the convex top of the machine were heat reflecting shields.

The possibilities of Die Glocke are limitless, thought Hitler. *I can send assassins back in time to eliminate Stalin, or Churchill, or Roosevelt.*

"Very well," said Hitler. "Well done."

General Hans Kammler breathed a sigh of relief.

PRESENT DAY

Only the brave find glory, the rest are forgotten by time.

Aeschylus
524 — 456 BC
Greek Playwright and Soldier

CHAPTER ONE

NIGHTMARES

It was just after three o'clock in the morning.

A time referred to as the Devil's Hour.

Lin Sparrow tossed and turned in her bed.

Sweat was beading on her forehead.

A low guttural moaning noise emanated from her throat and pushed through her lips.

Lin was asleep and dreaming.

It was the identical dream, night after night.

The dream always started the same way.

Lin was with James Ross, her fiancé. They were inside the Ministry of Science and Technology building in 1945 Berlin. Sounds of battle were echoing through the colossal marble foyer, and the overhead chandeliers were shaking. They walked down the foyer and came upon the entrance doors. Ross pulled the seventeen-foot-tall mahogany double doors open. What greeted them outside was unbelievable.

The scene was utter chaos. Berlin was indeed under siege from the First Belorussian Front commanded by Russian Marshall Zhukov. Smoke from artillery rounds filled the sky and streets. Buildings were burning. Small arms fire could be heard sporadically. Ross and Lin hurried down the concrete steps and took refuge behind what appeared to be a downed Panzer tank in front of the Ministry's steps.

"This is incredible," said Ross.

Ross saw an STG 44 Sturmgewehr assault rifle lying next to the body of a Wehrmacht soldier. He picked it up and turned the body over searching for other weapons. Ross pulled a Walther P-38 pistol out of the man's belt holster.

"Here," said Ross as he handed the Walther to Lin. "Let's move to the other side."

Ross and Lin walked around the Panzer tank, keeping low, and saw a young boy in the fetal position clutching his rifle. The boy was wearing an SS uniform indicating he was an Unterscharführer, or sergeant. The boy was surrounded by the bodies of his dead comrades.

Christ, thought Ross. *He's just a kid.*

Ross knelt down and touched the boy on the shoulder.

"Hey," said Ross.

The boy immediately jumped up and started flailing at Ross with his fists.

"Take it easy son, take it easy," said Ross as he held the boy's arms. Tears were streaming down the boy's face, but then he suddenly recognized the language Ross had spoken.

"You, you are Englander?" asked the boy between sobs.

Ross shook his head. "No. American."

Lin reached over and wiped the tears off the boy's face.

Ross asked, "What's your name?"

The boy said, "I am Ansgar Nachtnebel." He was trembling with fear. "I'm in the 3rd SS Panzer Division Totenkopf."

Ross noticed the boy was wearing an Iron Cross on his uniform.

That's the medal for bravery in combat, thought Ross.

"How old are you?" asked Lin.

Ansgar said, "Eleven."

Lin asked, "And how long have you been a soldier?"

"Four months," said Ansgar.

Ross looked at the bodies that the boy was surrounded by. They'd been shot to pieces. Some were missing legs and arms. Some were missing heads. Then he noticed the bodies in the street. Civilians. Many women. Old and young. Kids. They'd been sexually assaulted and butchered by the Red Army.

"How long ago did the Russians come through here?" asked Ross.

The boy was still shaking. "A couple hours ago."

KA-POW!

KA-POW!

KA-POW!

KA-POW!

Ross pushed Lin and Ansgar to the ground behind the Panzer tank. He scanned the street and saw several Russian soldiers walking towards them, shooting at various corpses.

Ross whispered, "Four Russian soldiers, coming this way."

Lin pulled back the slide on the Walther P-38, making sure a round was chambered.

"They're mopping-up," said Ross. "Just stay down. I've got this."

Ross leveled his Sturmgewehr across the rear fender of the Panzer. He sighted in on the four Russian soldiers. Then he flicked the selector switch to semi-auto for more controllability.

KA-POW!

First, Ross shot the furthermost Russian soldier — in the chest.

KA-POW!

Then Ross shot the closest Russian of the team — in the face.

Now the Russians reacted and wondered who was shooting at them and from where.

KA-POW!

Ross shot the next Russian in the team.

The last Russian soldier made a break for it and started to run away.

KA-POW!

KA-POW!

Ross shot him twice in the back.

Ansgar had been watching Ross.

Standing up, Ross said, "Okay it's over."

Lin helped Ansgar up.

"Are you all right?" asked Lin.

Ansgar had tears in his eyes.

He hugged Ross and said, "You saved my life! I'll never forget what you did! Those Russians surely would have killed us! You saved our lives!"

Ross wrapped his arm around Ansgar's shoulders and said, "It's okay, it's okay. It's all over now."

Ansgar looked up into Ross's face.

Why is this man so good? he thought.

Ross asked, "Do you have a home to go to?"

Ansgar shook his head. "No. Dead. They're all dead. My father is a soldier somewhere. I haven't seen him in seven months. My mother …"

Ansgar started to tremble again.

"… the Russians took my mother with them. I never saw her again. And my little sister was …"

Tears came streaming down Ansgar's cheeks.

"My little sister was …"

Lin embraced Ansgar.

"It's all right, it's all right," said Lin.

Ross knew he and Lin had to get back — back to the future — back to their future.

Ross placed both his hands on Ansgar's shoulders and said, "You have to go home now. Get out of here. Your obligation to the military is over. The war is lost. You must go home."

Ansgar said, "But I have no home, not anymore."

The noise from the heavy Russian artillery was getting closer and closer.

Ross unbuckled his Benrus Type 1 watch and placed it on Ansgar's wrist.

"Here," said Ross. "I want you to have this."

Ansgar looked at the watch and held it to his ear.

"Now," said Ross, "you have to go.   Keep going until you are safe."   Then Ross began to remember his World War Two history. "Head west," said Ross.   "Find the Americans or British.   Turn yourself over to them. They will take care of you." Then Ross shook hands with Ansgar.

Lin gave Ansgar a hug and kissed him on the cheek.

Ross turned to Lin and said, "Come on." He took her by the hand and headed back to the Ministry of Science and Technology building.

Ansgar watched them leave.

Then he picked up his Mauser rifle, took aim, and shot Ross in the back.

Noooooooooooooo!

Lin Sparrow awoke at five o'clock in the morning with the jolt of an electric spark.

Her nude body was glistening from head to toe with trickles of hot salty sweat.

She looked over at James Ross.

Still asleep.

So as not to awaken him, she delicately peeled off the thin white bedsheet that had been covering her, and tiptoed carefully into the small bathroom.

For the past two days they both had been staying in one of the spare bedroom living quarters on the second floor of Emanuel's place in Zurich Switzerland.

Emanuel was the enigmatic Philippine taxicab driver who had shared many of their past adventures.

Founded by the Romans just over two thousand years ago, Zurich has a population of almost two million, making it the largest city in Switzerland. It is one of the world's busiest economic financial centers as it has its own stock exchange. Its low tax rate draws many overseas corporations to position their headquarters there. The city is a plethora of culture, boasting festivals, art galleries, museums, symphonies, theater, opera, ballet, and multiple sporting events. Zurich is also the richest metropolitan area in Europe, and the world's largest gold bullion trading center. It's the home of many 5-star luxury hotels and restaurants, one in particular being the Asiatisches Essen Philippine Restaurant.

German for "Asian Food," *Asiatisches Essen* was owned by Emanuel's cousin Lailani and her husband Lars. Emanuel had lived in a room on the second floor, and after consulting with his cousin, allowed Ross and Lin to board in one of the other spare upstairs bedrooms. But Emanuel was gone now, having mysteriously vanished while piloting the Horten 229 V9 over the Bahamian Island of Abaco.

Lin clicked on the lights and examined her face in the large mirror hanging above the ancient porcelain sink.

This is crazy.

I've had the same dream, over and over now, for two nights.

Something is up.

Something is going to happen to us.

I can see it.

I can feel it.

I know it.

My mother said I was a seer.

She knew these dreams were more than nightmares or visions.

They were memories of a coming future.

Lin stared deeply into the brown eyes analyzing her in the mirror.

She picked up a tube of minty Colgate toothpaste and squeezed a dab out onto her pink toothbrush. Brushing her teeth quickly, Lin then gargled with an AAFES antiseptic mouthwash, courtesy the local Base Exchange, and spat the residue out into the sink. She walked over to the shower stall and slid open the transparent glass door, stepped inside, and then closed the door behind her.

With hot water jets pulsating, Lin scrubbed herself in the steamy shower with wild cherry blossom Suave deep moisturizing bodywash and lathered her hair with strawberry TRESemmé moisturizing shampoo. She thoroughly rinsed herself off with tepid water, and then stepped out of the shower. Grabbing a brown terrycloth towel, she dried herself off.

Back in the bedroom, Lin put on a sheer pair of panties and matching bra. Then she stepped into the new blue jeans which Ross had just bought her, and pulled on a Wimbledon white blouse. She slipped a two-baht gold chain with matching Buddha around her neck, and strapped a stainless steel Citizen Eco-drive ProMaster Dive watch with black rubber strap onto her left wrist. She splashed Obsession eau de parfum on her neck, and rubbed her wrists together with a dash.

Lin sat down on the bed and looked at herself in the bedroom mirror.

She was five feet nine inches tall.

That was tall for a Malaysian lady.

But Lin was only half Malay.

She was a mixture of East and West, just like her American boyfriend Captain James Ross.

Lin's mother, Mira Wan Tengku, was Malay, and her father, Lieutenant Alastair Jasper Sparrow, had been a British Special Air Service officer assigned to their embassy in Kuala Lumpur. He was killed from a terrorist bomb explosion when Lin was just a child. She had never really gotten to know her father all that well. Her mother never remarried, and had kept the last name of Sparrow.

Lin was twenty-six years old now.

She continued staring at herself in the mirror.

Her silky raven locks cascaded slightly below her shoulders, with bangs that stopped just above her eyebrows. She had long sexy eyelashes, and a petite nose that was slightly upturned. Her eyes were deep dark hazel pools that sparkled in the light, and her mouth was large and captivatingly beautiful, with glistening full lips. Her skin was very smooth with almost no body hair. As with most Asian women, her legs were naturally satiny smooth and never required shaving. She kept her fingernails cut short and unpainted, however she did apply a clear polish to her toenails. Her calves were muscled, her stomach flat, and at times she exhibited unusual strength.

Lin reached over to the nightstand and picked up a cosmetic brush to apply a little rouge blush powder to her half European cheeks.

When she was done, she looked around and slipped her feet into a pair of blue Asics running shoes.

Lin used to serve as Executive Personal Secretary to the Honorable Simon Watlington, the United States Ambassador to Malaysia. That was also when she first met James Ross. That civil service job had been rewarding, but at a cost to her dignity and self-respect. It just became too unbearable for her to work at the US Embassy in Kuala Lumpur. She simply could not stand to work, day after day, within the labyrinth of backstabbing political machinations. Lin had always wanted a job that she could be proud of. She wanted to do something that would make a difference in people's lives. She wanted to have a sense of actually helping people, of making the world a little better place to live in. She wanted to give something of herself back to the people of Malaysia. Consequently, she enrolled in an accelerated evening studies program at the Puteri Nursing College, and completed her Bachelor of Science in Nursing degree. She served for a time as a registered nurse in the emergency room of the Twin Towers Medical Center for Doctor Arjinderpal Sekhon in Kuala Lumpur, Malaysia. But then she started to have more dreams and visions — dreams and visions which included her then-boyfriend, James Ross, and which led to more and more adventures. Adventures which carried her across the globe and literally into and out of the jaws of death. And then Ross had proposed marriage, and she had accepted.

Lin heard a rustle of sheets behind her and glanced in the mirror to see Ross getting up.

"Guten Morgen meine Liebe," said James Ross, stretching out his arms and yawning.

Lin turned and wrapped her arms around Ross's neck and kissed him passionately. He responded and placed his hands on her waist.

"Good morning my love," purred Lin.

Lin looked into the deep pools of James Ross's piercing dark brown eyes.

Am I really engaged to this man?

She looked at the shards of hair hanging across his forehead that would never stay in place.

Is this for real?

Am I really here?

She looked at the lips that had always spoken the truth to her and satisfied herself that *yes,* this was indeed real and happening.

She had to be sure, since just last week she had been in Berlin Germany in 1945, having been transported there by Ross in Die Glocke — the Bell — the Nazi time machine. Their machine had short circuited after being hit by a Rocket Propelled Grenade (RPG) fired by a team of Chinese assassins and had returned to the past. But they had found another Die Glocke inside the Ministry of Science and Technology in 1945 Berlin. And now here they were back in Zurich.

Why did I love this man? pondered Lin.

James has always been troubled by the despair he sees in the world.

He has always been troubled when he sees good people suffer.

He has always been troubled when he sees evil doers triumph.

James sought out the answers from his faith.

His is the Christian faith.

His is the belief in the Christian God.

He questions why God would allow atrocities to occur rampant and flourish throughout the world.

Why does God allow innocents to be savagely raped and butchered?

Why does God allow children to be abused by the very institutions sworn to protect them and give them hope?

Why does God allow the existence of murder and war, disease and famine, injustice and evil?

Why does God allow his greatest creation — human beings — to die?

James's faith is a great mystery to him.

His faith promises salvation if you just believe.

But what James Ross came to understand, is that belief is not enough.

He realized that a human being has to act.

He realized that a human being has to create justice, seek truth, practice compassion, and gain wisdom.

Most importantly, James realized that a human being has to act with love.

He realized there were three questions to answer in life:

What is worth dying for?

What is worth living for?

What is most precious in the world?

To James Ross, the answer he found was always the same.

The answer —

— is love.

Lin was now engaged to James Ross.

Mr. and Mrs. James Ross, she mused.

He was an officer in the United States Army.

We should be planning our wedding.

We should be looking forward to a life together.

Together.

Forever.

Lin thought for a second …

She knew Ross was twenty-nine years old.

He's really tall too, probably six-foot-three I would guess, and around a hundred and eighty-five pounds or so.

With lovely piercing dark brown eyes, and sexy shards of brown hair hanging across his forehead that would never stay in place.

He was half Thai, half caucasian.

He was a Captain in the Special Forces.

He saved my life.

And I love him.

Oh I love him so.

Ross squinted at the luminescent dial of the alarm clock on the nightstand.

It was 0530 hours.

He stood up and staggered nude into the bathroom, flicking on the lights and fan. He didn't really need anyone to wake him up. As usual, he had mentally egressed himself to wake up through the sheer force of his will.

Ever since he had attended the Special Forces Qualification Course at Fort Bragg, he could just somehow *will* his body to wake up at anytime.   It wasn't magical.   It was just something that many SF soldiers were capable of doing.

Ross walked over and slid open the transparent glass doors of the shower stall and stepped in, closing them behind him.

Pulling the plastic power jet handles outward, he straightened his arms and leaned forward, pressing both of his palms against the shower wall under the needling spray.   Slowly, he lowered his head and allowed the heavy stream of hot pulsating water to cascade over his lean muscular body.

Ross completed the shower in his usual four minutes. He stepped out of the shower stall and wrapped one of the brown terrycloth towels around his waist.   The small tag on the towel read, "Troop Towel, Bath, Brown." Ross smiled.

Wiping his right hand across the steam covered mirror, he looked at himself.

He fingered his mornings worth of stubble and reached for his AAFES shave gel.   With a liberal amount of Army-Air-Force-Exchange-Services shave gel on, he slowly glided his razor across his face.   He lowered his head towards the sink and splashed hot water across his face to rinse off the remaining residue.   As if on cue, he poured Aqua Velva aftershave into his cupped left hand and slapped it on his face. Now he was awake.

Ross sauntered to the closet and pulled out his clothes.   His traveling ensemble was pretty much the same always. He stepped into a pair of red plaid boxer shorts.   Then he put on a white cotton shirt with tiny burgundy pinstripes running vertically. He cinched the collar with a narrow black necktie with a four-in-hand knot. Then he pulled on a black pair of pants with a black leather belt, black stretch socks, and stepped into his black leather shoes. And he topped it all off with his black suit coat.

Ross took a quick glance at himself in the bedroom mirror. He ran a comb through the thick shards of dark brown hair hanging across his forehead that would never stay in place. They just fell right back down again.

The hell with it, smiled Ross.

Ross came over and sat next to Lin on the bed. He delicately reached out, taking both her hands in his, and kissed them.

Lin nervously fingered the engagement ring Ross had given her. It was a one carat diamond, set in a four prong eighteen-karat gold ring.

"Darling, I have something very important to tell you," said Lin.

Ross had already guessed. "The dreams, isn't it? It's the dreams again."

"That's right," said Lin. "I've just had the same one again this morning."

Ross knew better than to question Lin Sparrow's dreams. They had always turned out to be metaphors for the truth. They were in fact visions of a possible future. A future, that if not changed, if not acted upon, would materialize as the present. And the visions had always saved his life by bringing Lin to him.

"What was the latest one, the one this morning?"

Lin stood up and started pacing about. She told Ross about the dream.

"Oh boy," said Ross. "And what?"

Lin looked at Ross with desperate eyes.

"And we were both in trouble from the young German soldier."

"I see," said Ross.

Lin said, "Even after you saved his life, he turned on us."

Ross looked into Lin's eyes. He had to change the subject.

"You know what," said Ross, "I'm hungry. Let's put the visions on hold for a bit and let me call Lailani. Maybe we can grab some breakfast. What do you say?"

"Okay. Breakfast sounds good," said Lin.

Ross picked up the Samsung Galaxy Stratosphere II that he had purchased from a local vendor in Berlin at the Tempelhof Park. He opened up his contacts and scrolled through until he found Lailani's number. Then he pressed the *call* button.

Bzzz.

Bzzz.

Bzzz.

Picking up her phone, Lailani pressed the little green *accept call* button and responded.

"Guten Morgen," said Lailani.

"Good morning Lailani. I'm sorry to disturb you so early."

"No, not at all James. What can I do for you?" asked Lailani.

Ross said, "I can smell your wonderful coffee way up here. Do you think Lin and I could come down and grab a cup?"

"I'll do you one better," said Lailani. "Lars and I have been preparing breakfast for you two. Why don't you come right down and dig in?"

"Bless you Lailani. You really are an angel," replied Ross.

Lailani said, "Come on down then. See you in a bit."

Ross was getting ready to hang up his phone when Lailani spoke once again.

"Oh and James ..." said Lailani.

"Yeah?"

"I noticed that 'the thing' is back in our garage again."

CHAPTER TWO

WHITE HOUSE BRIEFING

A crunchy glistening blanket of wet snow from the night before fell and transformed Lafayette Park along with the South Lawn into a Dickens frosty winter wonderland. Washington DC was beautiful this time of year for those who worked around the clock to secure freedom. The seat of power for that freedom is in the Executive Branch of the United States, otherwise known as the Office of the President. Since the Presidency of John Adams in 1800, the official residence of every Chief Executive has been the White House.

Located at 1600 Pennsylvania Avenue NW in Washington DC, the White House complex includes the Executive Residence, the East Wing, the West Wing, the Eisenhower Executive Office Building, and a guest residence known as Blair House. The President's Executive Residence has six stories, two of which are underground. The first floor of the West Wing includes the famous Oval Office, from which the President conducts most of his sensitive work.

The interior furnishings and seating arrangements can vary, but in the Oval Office today there were two large three-seat beige sofas facing each other and parallel to the President's famous Resolute Desk. This morning the Oval Office was a flurry of classified activity.

Executive Order 13526 had established the US classification information system.   Top Secret is the highest level of classified information there is. To publicly reveal Top Secret information is said to cause grave harm to the national security. Even certain Top Secret information is further broken down into Sensitive Compartmented Information, or SCI. This type of information can be openly reviewed inside a Sensitive Compartmented Information Facility, or SCIF. The Oval Office meets this strict criteria. It is not uncommon for classified information to be kept close-hold for various reasons — many of them political. Information is power, or so it is said.

Spread out on the couches facing each other were four of President Donald Trump's most trusted colleagues. They were: Counselor to the President, Metta Ngernluan, Director of the Central Intelligence Agency (CIA) Anna Kliner, Director of the National Security Agency (NSA) Teresa Cenni, and Chief of Staff of the Army General Braxton Matthews.

Metta Ngernluan's family legally immigrated to the United States from Laos when she was only two years old. Her father taught physics at Central Michigan University, and her mother was an accomplished concert pianist. Metta became a piano virtuoso by the age of five, and graduated magna cum laude from Harvard Law School at the age of twenty-three. She resigned as Team Chief of the Law Division of the Ford Motor Company when President Trump came calling. Metta was happy with her choice. She found President Trump to be a most engaging, sincere, and honest leader who used common sense.

"Thank you all for coming today. Let's just start with Metta, okay?" said the President.

The Counselor to the President cleared her throat.

"Sir," said Metta, "Elon Musk will meet with you this afternoon at 1300 hours. He will brief you on current DOGE (Department of Government Efficiency) cuts to the budget for USAID. He also has a proposal to revamp the tax code to eliminate income taxes for anyone making less than $150,000 per year. At 1400 hours Secretary of State Rubio will see you over Ukraine. At 1500 hours Secretary of Defense Hegseth will brief you on the new F-47 jet fighter, and at 1600 hours Director Gabbard will brief you on her efforts to consolidate intelligence dissemination."

President Trump was leaning forward in his chair and was, as usual, listening intently and with complete focus.

"Okay. Full day. Go on," he said.

"Yes sir. Border czar Tom Homan reports that the remainder of the border wall has been installed, and coupled with our zero-tolerance policies the Border Patrol is now reporting less than five illegal crossings per month," said Metta proudly.

"Great," replied the President. "I knew it. We can live with five but not five thousand like under Biden."

Metta smiled. "Yes sir."

"Crime is down 63% in Republican governed states since you last addressed the nation."

President Trump asked, "And what's going on in New York and

California?"

Metta looked at her spreadsheet.

"Unfortunately Governors Newsom and Hochul's policies remain the same. Smash and grab crime is pretty much rampant, and violent crime is up."

"Yeah," said President Trump, "such a shame. They need new governors that's all."

Metta smiled and said, "The strategic oil reserves have been refilled, and the Democrats are screaming that it is only benefiting oligarchs."

Trump chuckled.

"The price of oil is down 57%, and gasoline is at a national average of $1.87 per gallon. Your tax cuts are working and spending is up.   Businesses are coming back in droves to the US to establish residences. Everyone wants to manufacture here to avoid the tariffs. Inflation has reached an all time low of 1.2%."

President Trump smiled.

Metta reached for the manila folder on her lap with the red Top Secret coversheet and flipped it open.

"Sir," she said, "I'd like to now discuss Operation *Timeless Goddess* please."

President Trump leaned back in his chair and looked at the stack of folders flowing out of his *In Box*. He extracted the top one labeled *Timeless Goddess* and flipped it open.   The President was always amused at the code names used for operations.

"Mmm," mused President Trump, "uh-huh."

He looked at Metta and asked, "What about Captain Ross? Is he all right? I want to bring him to the White House to decorate him. What have we heard from him?"

Braxton Matthews spoke up.

"Sir I can answer that."

President Trump looked over at General Matthews.

Four-star General Braxton Matthews graduated at the top of his class from West Point. He was a career Special Forces officer, with multiple worldwide command and staff tours. Matthews had impressed President Trump so much by his initiatives to eradicate the ISIS caliphate that Trump made him his Army Chief of Staff. His experience with intelligence organizations was that they were interconnected by a surprisingly delicate structure, and loathed interfacing with each other to share information. US intelligence had become an intricate web where one hand didn't know what the other hand was doing. Information was provided too late or not at all. He swore to himself that if ever given the chance he would provide accurate information and as timely as possible.

Matthews said, "If you remember sir, Captain Ross secured the Spear of Destiny after the Chinese Team attempted to steal it, and he alerted us to the threat against your life and that of President Xi Jinping in Vienna last week."

President Trump said, "I remember. That's why I never got the chance to decorate him. I was too busy with Xi and too busy with the Secret Service." He threw the Top Secret folder on top of the Resolute desk and leaned back in his chair.

"Where is the time travel mechanism now?" asked the President.

Matthews said, "Sir, we believe Captain Ross has secured it in his possession."

Trump said, "We believe? You mean we're not sure?"

Matthews glanced around the room at his colleagues looking for assistance.

Teresa Cenni spoke up. "Yes Mister President, we believe Ross has secured Die Glocke."

NSA Director Teresa Cenni was a graduate of the University of Hawaii. A former surfer turned career US Navy Signal Corps officer, she still wore the Bulova surfboard chronograph watch with orange Swiss Tropic strap that her parents had given her for her twenty-fifth birthday. Teresa Cenni was named after her great grandmother, La Contessa Teresa di Cenni, whose claim to fame was that her husband, Santino, was the first to open a Bugatti dealership in Milan. Teresa had made a name for herself in the satellite and imagery field, and had retired at the rank of Vice Admiral. Shortly thereafter she was appointed by President Trump as his personal choice for NSA Director.

"Look," said the President, "this is the fourth briefing I've received on this Die Glocke, or Bell, or whatever the hell it is. Does it really function? I mean, does the damn thing work?"

NSA Director Teresa Cenni tried to reassure the President.

"Sir," said Teresa, "let me start from the beginning."

Teresa started to read from the folder in her hands.

"Sir, back in 1944 when the Third Reich was falling apart, SS-Obersturmbannführer Otto Skorzeny had entrusted his colleague, Obersturmführer Wilhelm von Lugoff, to safeguard Die Glocke. Die Glocke was actually designed to open a portal through time itself. It was a type of transporter to the past or the future. Through testing, Die

Glocke was found to be able to transfer a man into the fourth dimension. It appears sir, that it *was* in fact a time machine."

President Trump stared intensely at his NSA Director.

"Sir, the Nazis planned enormous military applications for Die Glocke. The idea was to transport select troops into the time vortex to conduct military operations that would guarantee total victory and win the war for Germany. A certain General Hans Kammler had been the engineer in charge of the V-2 missiles, and had been personally chosen by Himmler to lead the Nazi time travel project. It's even believed that his complete disappearance at the end of the war had something to do with the machine. Some said he transported himself to the future, and then returned the Bell back to the past. It has been chronicled in a scrub of our classified National Archives files that the Bell was actually responsible for the Kecksburg Pennsylvania UFO incident. Sir, this information has all been verified through our high surveillance satellite platforms including RAMPART, PRISM, OAKSTAR, and MYSTIC."

Trump thought for a second. "Okay, that's all well and good, but when will we have possession of it?" asked the President. "A machine with that potential cannot be left to chance."

CIA Director Kliner raised her arm.

Anna Kliner was a former military brat. She was the honor graduate in her Air Force ROTC class at Yale University, and received her commission as an Intelligence officer. She served for over thirty years and retired as a Lieutenant General, with her final assignment being as Director of the Defense Intelligence Agency (DIA) on Joint Base Anacostia-Bolling in Washington DC. President Trump had been impressed with her intelligence reports proving that the COVID-19 virus was actually specifically engineered and weaponized militarily as a bio-weapon, and that China had deliberately released it through its civilian airline travelers to crash world economies and, hopefully, crash President Trump's reelection bid. China hated Trump's tariffs, trade restrictions, and tough military posturing in the Pacific. They wanted him gone. So it was no surprise to anyone that President Trump appointed Anna as his CIA Director.

"Sir, if you remember there were four teams in Vienna last week. They were either attempting to acquire the Longinus Spear or the Die Glocke machine."

"Four?" asked President Trump. "Who were they again?"

"A Diplomatic Security Team which we sent, two Chinese Teams, and a Mossad Team."

"And how do we know that?" asked the President.

Anna said, "Sir, two weeks ago there was an attempt in Zurich to locate a certain Lin Sparrow, who we believe is the girlfriend of Captain James Ross.   The Chinese sent a team, and so did Israel. There was a gunfight. Two members of the Chinese Team were killed. They have been positively identified as members of the MSS."

President Trump raised an eyebrow and asked, "MSS?"

Anna said, "The Chinese Ministry of State Security.   It's their principal intelligence, national security, and secret police agency. After that, Lin Sparrow departed Zurich and ended up in Vienna with Captain Ross. We assume they both stopped the Chinese Team from stealing the Spear of Destiny. Then our information becomes a little sketchy. It appears that during the action, Captain Ross was hurt and ended up in a hospital. The medical team who worked on him were in fact also members of the MSS. And again this is somewhat sketchy and unverified, but it appears that Ross and Lin Sparrow eliminated this threat as well."

President Trump thought for a second. "Two tough cookies."

Anna said, "We feel that Captain Ross in fact does have possession of the sole surviving example of the Nazi time travel mechanism."

"Well what the hell happened to our DSS Team?" asked President Trump. "Why didn't they secure Die Glocke?"

Anna said, "It appears sir, that the Israeli Team intercepted them and stopped them. Our team leader, Special Agent Erwin Foxwell, reported that the Israeli Team seemed to know Lin Sparrow."

"When you say Israeli Team, you mean a Mossad Team, right?" asked the President.

"Yes sir."

"Mossad is very good at everything they do. Remember the exploding pagers they sent Hamas leaders? How does a Mossad Team end up knowing Lin Sparrow?" asked the President.

Teresa Cenni spoke up. "Sir, it's possible that Lin Sparrow is a member of Mossad."

General Braxton Matthews stared at the NSA Director. This was information he was hearing for the very first time.

President Trump wasn't fazed by it. "I hope she is. Old Bibi Netanyahu is a great friend of mine. I trust him. This could turn out to be a joint mission. Is there any chance that Lin Sparrow secured the machine?"

Teresa said, "Sir, satellite imagery from last week showed the machine in a field next to a parking lot at the Burggarten."

The Burggarten is a park next to the Hofburg. It originally was a Napoleonic battlefield in the early 1800s. The park is full of statues and monuments. There's even a Mozart statue which has a whole labyrinth of tunnels beneath it. The Hofburg was built in the thirteenth century and is located in the center of Vienna. It is the former imperial palace of the Habsburg Dynasty. Today, the Hofburg Palace is the official workplace and residence of Austrian President Alexander Van der Bellen. Part of its 59 acreage houses the museum, with 21 rooms filled with rare antiquities dating back thousands of years. Some of these include imperial treasures of the Holy Roman Empire, ecclesiastical artifacts of emperors, and jewel encrusted crowns of former kings and queens. The Spear of Destiny is also located there on public display.

"Was it there when I was meeting with Xi Jinping last week at the Austrian Parliament?" asked President Trump.

"Yes sir. It was across the street at the Hofburg field, covered in snow. We have imagery of Captain Ross and Miss Sparrow getting into it, and then it disappeared."

Trump asked, "What do you mean disappeared?"

"After Ross and Sparrow got into it, the machine started to glow, and then vanished. It disappeared," said Teresa.

General Matthews said, "Well that must mean it works."

President Trump picked up a pen from his desk and started writing inside his *Timeless Goddess* folder. After a few seconds he asked, "Okay, is Ross safe?"

General Matthews replied, "Sir, I tried to contact him this morning but got no response. I'll keep trying again after this meeting. As soon as I find out I'll let you know, sir."

President Donald Trump studied the four faces of his most trusted staff officers sitting in from of him.

"Braxton, I want you to monitor this Ross situation very closely. I trust Captain Ross. Is he a Republican?" said President Trump self-mockingly.

Everybody laughed.

"Yes sir," replied General Matthews smiling. "I'm sure he is."

Trump smiled. "And Anna, it's fine if Mossad is in on this. Let's work together. Joint interoperability. But the United States wants that machine for our own national security," said the President.

"Roger that sir."

"All of you coordinate. I want to know everything that is going on with this time travel device, and I want it secured by our people as soon as possible. To me, it sounds like Captain Ross has it in his possession already."

The trusted advisors all nodded simultaneously.

"Keep me informed. Okay, that's it for now," said President Trump.

The four staff officers rose to attention and followed the president out of the Oval Office.

CHAPTER THREE

REVELATIONS

Zermatt is beautiful at midnight.   The lights from the village provide a warm, soft, comforting glow in direct contrast to the icy cold omnipotence of the Alps. Zermatt is a town in the canton of Valais in Switzerland. With a population around six thousand, Zermatt is world-renown as a mountaineering and ski resort that sits at the foot of the Matterhorn.   Nestled just outside Zermatt, on twenty prime acres of real estate, is the compound of billionaire Ansgar Ludwig Nachtnebel.

Nachtnebel was feeling every one of his ninety-one years today. He had been informed through his intelligence contacts that his plan to eliminate the presidents of China and the United States had failed. Along with that, all members of both Chinese Teams had been killed, and that his good friend Doctor Wu Qiang was among the dead. Ansgar stared out the panoramic window of his mountain mansion at the lights below in Zermatt.

Everything was set, he thought.

"Would you care for a nightcap, sir?" asked Aemilius Urs, his trusted manservant.

Nachtnebel turned around and said, "Yes, yes I would. Bring me a Napoleon brandy."

Aemilius bowed. "Very good sir."

Then he scurried off to fetch the brandy.

Nachtnebel walked into his library. The room held his vast collection of treasures, from Egyptian art to Mesopotamian artifacts. The walls were adorned with paintings from Picasso, Degas, and Matisse. His library walls housed first editions of Hemingway, Steinbeck, Fleming, Cervantes, Dostoevsky, and Hugo. But none of that meant anything to Ansgar, for this room also held his most treasured possession of all. The ownership of which made everything else of as little consequence. He walked over and stared at it in its glass display case.

Aemilius returned with the brandy and noticed his boss looking in the case.

"Would you care for me to remove it for you, sir?" asked Aemilius.

Nachtnebel said, "Yes. Bring it to me over by the fireplace."

Aemilius bowed and proceeded with his white-gloved hands to lift the glass covering and remove the object.

Nachtnebel seated himself in a plush red leather-bound chair next to the grand fireplace. The crackling fire brought back memories of his childhood growing up in Berlin.

Aemilius bowed and said, "Here you are sir." He placed the object into Nachtnebel's aged hands.

Nachtnebel looked at the watch. It was a Benrus. Not at all unusual, as Benrus watches have been around since 1921. But this watch was special. It had been given to him by the only human being who had ever done an unselfish act for him. It was given to him in April of 1945 by an American soldier. That soldier had saved his life from a Russian patrol in the streets of Berlin. A patrol that would have most certainly raped him before they killed him. This watch was very special indeed, as was the soldier who had given it to him those many years ago.

But this Benrus watch holds a secret, thought Nachtnebel.

He turned the watch over and looked at the inscribed date of manufacture.

NOV 2020.

Nachtnebel thought to himself, *How did an American soldier, during the siege of Berlin in 1945, give me a watch off his wrist with a manufacture date of over seventy-five years in the future?*

Nachtnebel said, "Aemilius, bring me the folder."

Aemilius hurried over with the manila folder. He placed it on the end table next to his employer.

"Here you are sir," said Aemilius.

Nachtnebel looked up at his servant.

"That will be all this evening, Aemilius," he said.

Aemilius bowed and hurried from the library, closing the twelve-foot-tall mahogany double doors behind him.

The library was dark except for the flickering flames in the large marble fireplace. They crackled and sizzled their obedient servitude.

Nachtnebel sipped his brandy and opened the folder. Inside was a Chinese MSS dossier on the man responsible for the failed attempt to steal the Longinus Spear at the Hofburg. This man was also accountable for the ruined plans to assassinate President Trump and President Xi Jinping in Vienna. This was the same man answerable for the deaths of two teams of Chinese MSS agents. But more than that, this man was responsible for the death of Nachtnebel's good friend, Doctor Wu Qiang.

He flipped through the pages and read about the man.

Ross, James B.

Twenty-nine years old.

Captain, US Army Special Forces.

Profession: American assassin.

Then Nachtnebel found his photographs.

He looked at the young handsome face with the hint of Asian heritage.

He looks like a handful, thought Nachtnebel. *Wait a second — I've seen this man before. I know I have! No! It couldn't be him!*

Then he picked up a magnifying glass from the end table and studied the photograph more closely.

Yes! It's him!

He flipped through more photos and saw one where the man had a watch on his wrist.

Nachtnebel bent closer with the magnifying glass and studied the wristwatch.

My God, it is! he thought. *This man is wearing a Benrus Type 1*

Class A dive watch. The same type of watch the American soldier gave me in 1945 in Berlin! The American who saved my life!

"Well I'll be goddamned," he said.

Then he bent over and studied the photographs more intensely.

Nachtnebel thought, *It surely is him. It's the same man. There can be no doubt. And the watch! The Benrus dive watch! It's the same.*

Talking to himself, Nachtnebel said, "But how? How can it be? How could he have been in 1945 and Vienna last week?"

Nachtnebel turned back to the front contents page of the dossier. He ran his finger down the contents until he found an entry labeled *Past Operations, p.12.* Then he quickly flipped through to page 12.

Scanning the page, Nachtnebel said, "Here it is. Here it is!" Then he read out loud: "US Army Captain James Ross is the main subject in the MSS investigation in the death of the People's Navy Rear Admiral Shui Gui in the Bahamas last month. Captain Ross is believed to have in his possession the Die Glocke machine."

So that's it, thought Nachtnebel. *That's how he did it. I've heard the stories, the myths. I thought they were wives tales told to frighten children. But it's true. It must be. It's all true. The Nazi's succeeded. That damned Kammler and Von Braun. They actually did it!*

Nachtnebel held up a picture of Ross in his hand and sneered. Then he talked to the photograph and said, "It doesn't matter that you saved my life all those years ago. I want that accursed machine. I'll use it to win the war before it starts, even if it means I kill you in the process, Captain Ross."

CHAPTER FOUR

RESOLUTIONS

Ross followed Lin down the creaking wooden staircase to the main floor kitchen area of the Asiatisches Essen Philippine Restaurant and sat down on one of the high barstools behind the stainless kitchen counter for breakfast.

Lialani had finished setting the counter and was piling food on it from the grill. There were stacks of bacon, Vienna sausages, French toast with Al Johnson's Swedish syrup, scrambled eggs, toast, and hash browns. Her husband Lars brought over a pitcher of ice cold orange juice and a steaming pot of black coffee.

"Good morning Lin. Good morning James," said Lailani.

Ross and Lin answered almost simultaneously, "Morning."

"Please, help yourself," said Lailani pointing to the breakfast.

Lailani and Lars sat opposite Ross and Lin, and everyone began heaping their plates with mounds of food.

Ross said, "Everything just looks great."

"It sure does," said Lin. "Thank you so much."

Lars said, "No problem."

After a few minutes of feasting, Lars said, "Tell me James, what are you going to do with the machine?"

Ross stared at him with a mouthful of hash browns.

"You know," said Lars, "with the machine in our garage."

Ross said, "Today, Lin and I are going to get rid of it. It will be gone today, that I can promise."

Lars said, "It seems to me this is the machine all the fuss is about, isn't it?"

"Yes," answered Ross.

Lailani asked, "What are you going to do with it?"

Ross and Lin looked at each other.

Lin said, "We're going to destroy it."

Lars took a sip of his coffee.

"But how?" asked Lars. Being a Swiss businessman, Lars saw the potential in selling the machine to a museum or historical society.

Ross said, "Leave that to me."

Secretly Ross was contemplating sinking Die Glocke in Lake Toplitz in the Salzkammergut district.

Lars looked at Lailani.

"We never pried much into Emanuel's life. But we do know he was working with the Israeli's. We've had his friends over many times. I believe you've met most of them — Zvi, Yitzhak, and the others."

Ross said, "Yes, we sure have."

Lin said, "And we're sorry we've disrupted your lives so much."

Lailani said, "No, no you haven't. You were good friends to Emanuel. He used to talk about you all the time."

Ross's Samsung cellphone came to life.

Bzzz.

Bzzz.

Bzzz.

"What the —?"

Ross stared at the number. He immediately recognized it as having the 703 area code of Arlington Virginia.

Ross remembered back to when he had thrown his US Army-issued Blackberry cellphone into the Limmat River in Zurich. That was after he had received a message on it to report back to the Warrior Transition Battalion at Fort Sam Houston Texas. Ross had been an inpatient convalescing there after the drone explosion which had incapacitated him. He had been ordered back because the US State Department reported that he had improperly used his diplomatic passport to enter Switzerland while on military leave — and they had turned him in. Somehow the Department of Defense had been able to track him again, even though he was now using a secondhand Samsung Galaxy Stratosphere II that he had purchased from a local vendor in Berlin at the Tempelhof Park.

Bzzz.

Bzzz.

Bzzz.

The Samsung continued to ring.

"Excuse me," said Ross. He stood up and slowly walked into the main dining area to have some privacy.

Ross pushed the *accept call* button and took the call.

"Hello?" he said.

There was a delay on the other end of the phone for a second.

"Hello?" said Ross.

"Jim Ross?" asked a voice. "Is this Jim Ross?"

Ross immediately recognized the familiar voice.

"Yes sir," he replied.

"Jim this is Braxton," said the voice. "Braxton Matthews."

It was Ross's old Special Forces Battalion Commander, Braxton Matthews. General Matthews was now the Chief of Staff of the United States Army.

"Yes sir," said Ross again.

"Where are you now?" asked General Matthews.

"Back in Zurich, sir."

Ross knew the SIPRNet was the Department of Defense Secret Internet Protocol Router Network. But he was not on the SIPRNet now. He was on an open line unsecured phone call.

General Matthews said, "Do you have the machine?"

A thousand reasons flooded into Ross's head about why he should lie. But his Special Forces friendship with Braxton Matthews told him not to.

"Yes sir," said Ross, "I do."

"All right. Message me your address and I'll arrange military transport and a State Department Team to pick it up and fly it out of Zurich, along with you. I'm flying you to Andrews and you'll meet the president. By the way, who is Lin Sparrow?"

Ross said, "She's my fiancée, sir."

General Matthews said, "Congratulations James! Then Lin has to come with you of course."

"Okay sir. That'll be great," said Ross.

General Matthews said, "Now here's what else is happening …"

CHAPTER FIVE

STORMBREW

Ansgar Ludwig Nachtnebel was feeling his age. At ninety-one years old, he knew he hadn't much time left on this earth. But he'd seen a lot. Oh yes, he'd seen a lot.

Nachtnebel grew up in Prussia, and witnessed the horrors of the economic depression that followed Germany's tragic loss in war. In 1944 at the tender age of eleven, young Nachtnebel became a member of the Hitler Youth in Berlin. He grew quite a reputation for himself by turning in the locations of suspected Jews to the Nazi Schutzstaffel, or SS. In early 1945, Nachtnebel joined the 3rd SS Panzer Division Totenkopf, and fought savagely during the defense of Berlin. He was awarded the German Cross for bravery on the same day it was announced that the Führer had been killed in the fighting. Nachtnebel was taken prisoner by General Patton's Third Army in May 1945, and served four months in an allied prisoner of war camp in Wickrathberg. Upon his release, he was repatriated to England in 1946, where he first found employment as a bank clerk, and later moved up to bank teller. By the age of twenty-five, he had become a stockbroker and was soon on his way up the financial ladder. When he turned forty-five, he established his own European monetary fund, and had assets valued at over one billion dollars. Nachtnebel was a master at accumulating and then manipulating a country's currency by *selling short*. Selling short means an investor borrows stock shares that he believes will drop in price, then he sells those borrowed shares at market price, then he buys back the shares when the price drops. Finally, he returns the shares to the original lender, profiting from the difference. He amassed millions in Thai baht and the Malaysian ringgit, and later sold them short and thus tripled his investments. Nachtnebel was accused of deliberately crashing the economies of several countries for his personal profit. But his answer was that when the currencies start to decline, he purchases them to realize profits later based on his speculation. Triggering monetary crisis for fun and profit became his mantra. As an atheist, Nachtnebel was only concerned with making more and more money. He was not concerned with how his tactics affected the lives of ordinary people. Today, he is the Director General of the Nachtnebel New World Institute, which speculates in radical Marxist-Leninist approaches to reorganizing worldwide international financial systems.

Ansgar Nachtnebel and Doctor Wu Qiang had met seven years ago at the World Psychotherapy Forum in Geneva, Switzerland. Nachtnebel was lecturing on his "Quantum Millionaire" theory that basically anyone, regardless of background, can become wealthy by selling short and betting on the future price of a stock. In Doctor Wu

Qiang, he found a kindred heart that believed mankind was in need of a reboot. Doctor Qiang found his financial backer. Together they devised a plan, fictitiously at first, that would bring the world superpowers to the brink of war. Someone who could speculate on such an event would be able to make billions of dollars. After several meetings in Geneva, they decided that what was needed was to get the United States and China's economies to outspend each other through war. Everything came together in Vienna with the Trump/Xi summit. The Chinese Teams were already in country with the Spear of Destiny mission, and all that was needed was the capture of an American soldier to be used as the patsy. Doctor Wu Qiang knew certain death awaited him in China if it should ever be revealed that he had a hand in this conspiracy. But, like his friend Ansgar, Wu was willing to take the gamble. He was willing to risk his life for capitalist gains. He was speculating.

As far as Ansgar Nachtnebel was concerned — he was old, he wanted more billions for his children, and he was safe in his secure fortress compound in Zermatt Switzerland. He firmly believed the world was due for a complete reboot as well. He was ready to make it happen. The one thing he didn't count on was the resiliency of Green Beret Captain James Ross.

Nachtnebel had been informed through his intelligence contacts that his plan to eliminate the presidents of China and the United States had failed. Along with that, all members of both Chinese Teams had been killed, and that his good friend Doctor Wu Qiang was among the dead. Nachtnebel stared out the panoramic window of his mountain mansion at the lights below in Zermatt.

He thought to himself, *Captain Ross it turns out, was the American soldier who saved my life during the Battle of Berlin those many years ago. His dossier photographs prove it. He gave me his Benrus watch back in 1945. I've been fascinated by it all these years because it is dated November 2020 on the back. That particular situation could only have manifested itself if Ross had Die Glocke, the Nazi time machine. There can be no other rationalization. I had heard bits and pieces from my Chinese friends that they were after it. Now I know it to be true. There can be no other explanation. There's only one thing to do,* he thought. *Captain Ross has interrupted my plans long enough. And he has Die Glocke! I need to get that machine. The possibilities to use it are endless.*

Nachtnebel picked up his cellphone and scrolled through his contacts. Then he placed a call.

Bringgg.

Bringgg.

Bringgg.

590 miles north in Magdeburg Germany, Erebus Stormbrew looked at his phone.

Hmm, he thought. *This could be interesting.*

He picked up his phone and answered.

"Yes, Mein Herr," said Stormbrew.

Nachtnebel asked, "Are you available for work?"

Stormbrew knew whenever Ansgar Nachtnebel called, big money followed.

"But of course, Mein Herr," Stormbrew answered. "I am at your disposal."

"Good, good," said Nachtnebel. "How soon can you be in Zermatt?"

Stormbrew said, "I can be there tonight Mein Herr."

Nachtnebel said, "Fine, fine. I'll send funds to your mobile wallet. And I'll have my people waiting at the airstrip to pick you up. They'll bring you straight to the house. I'll be expecting you."

"May I inquire as to the job, Mein Herr?" asked Stormbrew.

Nachtnebel responded cryptically, "I'll brief you tomorrow. Good night."

"Very well. Gute Nacht Mein Herr," said Stormbrew. Then he hung up his phone.

Erebus Stormbrew was forty-two years old. His father was a German Bundeswehr officer, and his mother was a Finnish ballerina. He was six-feet-four inches tall, and weighed a fit two-hundred-twenty pounds. Stormbrew sported a graying military-style crew cut, and had frosty blue-green eyes. Martial arts was his form of fitness, and he had the cauliflower ears to prove it. He was a black belt in Korean Taekwondo, having studied it for thirty years. He himself was a former captain in the Kommando Spezialkräfte (KSK) of the German Heer, until he struck a superior officer for what Stormbrew felt was an act of cowardice under fire. Stormbrew left the army and found it was much more lucrative to hire his services out. He also found it was much more profitable to smuggle heroin and fentanyl through the Corsican pipeline. He soon developed a reputation in Europe for doing "anything, anytime, anywhere." Stormbrew had created a relationship with Ansgar Nachtnebel when he successfully rescued his eldest son from kidnappers in Zimbabwe.

Stormbrew returned to his bedroom where his guest had been patiently waiting. Her name was Ludmela Dvořák. She was born in the Czech Republic. With short blonde hair and only twenty years old, Ludmela was five-foot-six and weighed a mere one-hundred-and-fifteen pounds. She had a very beautiful and strong body. Growing up as a farm girl, she got pregnant at the age of seventeen and was treated terribly by her boyfriend who refused to marry her. Raising a child was extremely difficult by herself in the city of Vyskov. She worked two jobs but it never seemed to be enough. She could only make small money working in restaurants. Finally she had to give her child up for adoption. After that she lost her self-esteem and became a professional escort. Her price was high because she allowed men to get a little rough with her.

Stormbrew only paid for the best since his tastes were quite different, quite rare. Stormbrew was the type of man who enjoyed hurting women. He was a sadist.

Ludmela was completely nude and on all fours on the bed. Her face was down and her buttocks jutted up. Stormbrew's excitement grew and he slapped her behind.

"Do you like it?" he asked.

Ludmela was trained to answer perverts in an agreeable manner.

"Oh yes. Give it to me, please," she said.

Stormbrew slapped her buttocks once again, this time very hard, which left a red hand impression.

"Do you want me?" he asked.

Ludmela squealed with faux delight, further enticing her client for the evening.

"Oh yes," lied Ludmela, "give it to me hard."

Stormbrew pulled down his shorts and thrust into her. He leaned over her and pushed her head down into the bed. With one hand on either side of her buttocks, he thrust deeper and harder. Sweat was beading on his forehead and chest. Then he grabbed a handful of her blonde hair and jerked her head back.

"You'll like the next part, Ludmela," seethed Stormbrew with his stinking breath on her face. Then he began to sodomize her.

Ludmela exclaimed, "Hey wait a minute! Stop!"

But Stormbrew jerked her head back by her hair even harder and continued to sodomize her over and over.

Stormbrew said between gritted teeth, "I thought this was what you wanted? Don't you like it?"

Ludmela had tears streaming down her cheeks now, and Stormbrew continued thrusting until he could see Ludmela was macerated. With Ludmela openly sobbing now, Stormbrew again pulled her by her hair around facing him so that she could now perform fellatio on him.

"Give it to me baby," said the wretched man.

When he finally climaxed, he released his hold of her hair and let her fall back to the bed. Stormbrew walked over to his bedroom closet and reached into the inner pocket of his suit coat. He extracted 900 euros and threw it on Ludmela's sweating nude body.

Stormbrew said matter-of-factly, "Time for you to leave. I've got to catch a flight now."

Ludmela snatched up the money and slowly got off the bed and put on her clothes.

As she was walking out of the apartment she thought, *I curse you mister. I curse you from this day forward. You will have bad luck all the remaining days of your life. I pray you get to feel the same pain you just gave to me. Goddamn you to Hell.*

CHAPTER SIX

DECISION TIME

After breakfast, Ross sat down with Lin upstairs in their bedroom and discussed what to do about Die Glocke.

"What do you think, Jamie?" asked Lin.

Ross said, "Yeah. It's a difficult decision. It could be a mistake to allow our government to take control of Die Glocke. I mean, how do we know they won't use it in a nefarious way?"

Lin said, "We don't. Maybe we should just give it to them and be done with it. But like you said, we could just as simply dump it in Lake Toplitz."

Ross answered, "Yeah."

"But how would you ever explain that to your General friend?" said Lin. "I mean, what would you tell him?"

Ross thought for a second. "If we dump it in the lake, it would have to be done clandestinely, without the government knowing. If they knew, then they would eventually be able to recover it."

"It's a dilemma all right," said Lin. "That machine is nothing but trouble."

Ross reached out and took Lin's hands in his.

"We have to give it to General Matthew's people," said Ross. "It's the best thing for us to do. He wants to fly the machine and us to Andrews Air Force Base in Maryland. We have to go. Supposedly we're going to meet the president too."

Lin said, "Okay. Then that's it. Have you already given him our address?"

Ross said, "No not yet. That's what I've got to do now."

Lin stood up from the bed and said, "Okay, while you're doing that I'm going to change my clothes for Maryland."

Ross pulled out his Samsung Galaxy Stratosphere II cellphone and sent General Matthews his physical address where to pick up Die Glocke.

One hundred miles away in Zermatt, Ansgar Nachtnebel was sitting in the information technology (IT) office of his compound and watching his people as they intercepted Ross's phone message.

"We have him sir," said Giovanni Gabriel, the director of the IT section. "We have the location of the pickup."

Nachtnebel said, "Excellent. Good work men."

Gabriel handed the printout to his boss and sat back in his chair.

Nachtnebel looked at the Zurich address for the Asiatisches Essen Philippine Restaurant. Then he handed the paper to the man sitting next to him.

"What do you think?" asked Nachtnebel.

Erebus Stormbrew took the paper and studied it. "It will be simple," he said. "It comes down to either killing everyone there and stealing the machine, or simply portraying ourselves as the team sent to pick up the machine. We just have to get there before the real team shows up. Either way, you'll have your Die Glocke."

PART TWO

The world breaks everyone, and afterward, many are strong at the broken places.

> Ernest Hemingway
> 1899 — 1961
> American Writer

CHAPTER SEVEN

SUBTERFUGE

Ross and Lin knew General Matthews was sending a State Department Team to pick up Die Glocke. Their mission was to transport the machine to the Zurich airport, along with Lin and Ross, and fly them all to Andrews Air Force Base. As Ross had discussed with Lin — there was no other choice — not if Ross wanted to remain an officer in the United States Army.

Ross said, "General Matthews says the team will be here this afternoon. They'll bring a transport flatbed and a crane."

Lin could read the thoughts of James Ross better than anyone. She knew he was deeply troubled by agreeing to turn over Die Glocke to the government. Although there appeared to be a common sense presidential administration in power now, that didn't mean there would always be one.

Lin said, "It's really the best thing to do. You've done all you could. No one could have done more."

Ross and Lin were sitting by one of the windows overlooking the parking lot of the Asiatisches Essen Philippine Restaurant and having coffee. They were keeping a sharp lookout for when the team would arrive. Lailani walked over and poured them some more coffee.

"I think you're doing the right thing," said Lailani. She looked at Ross's troubled face. She knew he didn't think so.

"Thanks Lailani," said Ross.

"Oh look," said Lailani staring out the window, "here comes something now."

Coming up the driveway was a Mercedes-Benz flatbed truck, followed by a Mercedes-Benz Arocs 3-axle tractor with heavy lift loading crane, and two black BMW i7 sedans.

"This must be them," said Ross standing up. "Let's go greet them."

Lon G. Inus was in his apartment on Mariahilfer Strasse. He had been up since dawn and was planning on visiting the Hofburg Palace Museum. He visited it daily. It was his sole routine. He stood for hours looking at the Longinus Spear. Also known as the Spear of Destiny and the Holy Lance, it was said to have mystical powers. Some claimed it was able to heal the sick, bring victory in battles, and even foretell the future.

Sporting classic good looks, Lon G. Inus appeared to be in his middle thirties, six-foot-two, 187 pounds, had shiny black hair always cut short, suntanned, and was extremely fit. The letters *SPQR* were tattooed on his left forearm. Most people thought he was Italian. Inus always dressed conservatively in a black suit with long black overcoat.

At a distance he looked like a young Sylvester Stallone. There was one thing about him that women found most endearing — his dark brown eyes — they always looked sad.

Lon G. Inus, otherwise known as Longinus, had buried his wife and daughters centuries ago. He had watched everyone he ever loved pass away. Through the two millennia he had already lived since that tragic day on Golgotha, the Centurian known as Longinus had come to realize that he was kept alive to protect the Spear of Destiny. His task was to safeguard the spear until the return of Jesus Christ.

That terrible vision I had last night, he thought, *I've got to call James and let him know.*

Bzzz.

Bzzz.

Bzzz.

Just then Ross's cellphone rang. He pulled it out and looked at it.

"Hmm," said Ross, "it's Longinus."

Handing the phone to Lin, Ross said, "Here, you take it."

Lin stood up and took the phone. She followed Ross outside while answering the phone.

"Hello Lon, this is Lin," she said.

Longinus said, "Hello Lin. Is James there? I've got to speak to him on a matter most urgent."

Lin looked at Ross. He was walking over and telling the team of State Department men where to pull their vehicles around to.

"He's kinda tied up at the moment," said Lin.

Longinus thought for a second.

"All right, then you've got to tell him. Don't let anyone move Die Glocke today," said Longinus.

"What?" exclaimed Lin. "Why?"

Longinus said, "I had a vision last night that there would be treachery in an attempt to move Die Glocke today. That it would come from someone who should have died long ago, and that this person has a tie to James from the past."

Lin was astonished. She believed whatever Longinus said was true, because she knew the truth about who he was, and what he was.

My God, she thought, *I've got to warn James.*

But it was too late.

Lin was still talking with Longinus when the caravan pulled around from the garage and circled back to the front parking lot of the restaurant. She noticed a huge object on the flatbed with a large gray tied-down tarpaulin covering it. Simultaneously, the two black BMW sedans pulled up. Ross and a tall man with a gray crew cut hairstyle and wearing a long black overcoat got out of one. They stood shaking hands. Ross saw Lin and waved for her to come over and join them.

Lin, thinking quickly, yelled, "I've got to go to the ladies' room," and waved.

I'll just text James about what's going on, she thought.

Lin started walking back to the restaurant while texting to Ross.

Dammit, she realized, *this is James's phone!*

Then Lin did an abrupt turnaround and started running to Ross and frantically waving her arms. She shouted, "Stop!"

Ross was surprised at first, then quickly turned around and looked at the man who had identified himself with US State Department credentials. But Erebus Stormbrew heard Lin yelling and was already shouting orders as he hurriedly got back into the BMW.

"Go!" yelled Stormbrew. Then he activated an M8 pyrotechnic smoke grenade and threw it at Ross.

Ross dropped to the pavement to allow the smoke to pass over him. The escape of the Mercedes trucks and the two speeding BMWs was concealed by the billowing choking white fumes.

CHAPTER EIGHT

OUT OF THE PAST

Ross got up and was coughing and backing away from the white smoke.

"What the hell is going on?" yelled Ross to Lin as she came running up to him.

Out of breath, Lin gasped, "I was just talking to Longinus. He warned me of an attempt to hijack Die Glocke today."

"What?" said Ross.

"That's right. He just told me he had a vision about someone who should have died long ago, with a connection to you, who would steal Die Glocke today. Here," said Lin dialing Longinus's number, "talk to him."

Ross took the phone and said, "Hello Lon? This is James. Lin just told me about your vision and …"

Longinus interrupted and said, "James, whatever you do, don't let Die Glocke out of your sight today."

Ross said, "It's too late. They took it. But who are they?"

Longinus said, "It's the billionaire named Ansgar Nachtnebel. He was the one behind the attempted theft of the Spear of Destiny, and the kidnapping of you."

Ross was stunned.

Ansgar? The eleven-year-old kid I met in Nazi Germany in 1945? thought Ross.

Longinus said, "You saved his life and gave him your watch. He's never forgotten you. Today, he's a billionaire philanthropist. He's an atheist who funds left wing causes which he has designed to bring down democracies and produce a collapse of societal values. He sows utter chaos. But now he knows you were the one who prevented the theft of the spear, and he thinks you killed his best friend, the Chinese Doctor Wu Qiang. He's been briefed on you. He's seen your pictures. He's tied the date on the back of your watch to the only plausible explanation — the existence of Die Glocke."

Ross listened carefully.

"Lon," said Ross, "do you know where they've taken the machine?"

Longinus replied, "To Zermatt Switzerland, at the foot of the Alps. Nachtnebel has a place there, a compound." Longinus thought for a second. "Actually it's like a fortress."

Ross continued talking to Longinus while he and Lin walked back into the restaurant. A stunned Lailani and Lars met them.

"My God," exclaimed Lars, "what is going on?"

Ross cupped the phone and said, "Give me a minute, Lon."

Then he attempted to explain the situation to Lars and Lailani.

When he was done, he returned his attention to the phone call.

"Okay Lon, I'm back," said Ross.

"Listen," said Longinus, "I'm coming out there to help you on this one."

Sitting down at a table with Lin inside the restaurant, Ross said, "But what about the spear?"

Longinus replied, "The spear can wait for me a couple of days."

Ross thought to himself, *Yeah I guess it can. Lon has been waiting for two thousand years.*

"All right," said Ross. "How soon can you be here?"

Longinus said, "The flight out of Vienna to Zurich is only just a little over an hour. I'll be there this afternoon. Are you staying at Emanuel's place in Zurich, the restaurant?"

Ross said, "Yes."

Longinus said, "Very well. See you soon." Then Longinus hung up.

Lailani walked over to the table with a pot of coffee.

"You both look like you could use some."

CHAPTER NINE

BLACK MAGIC

No airlines offer direct flights from Zurich to Zermatt. It takes approximately three-and-a-half hours to drive there, and Zermatt has the designation of being a car-free village. This is to minimize pollution, preserve the mountain environment, and support the town's quaint atmosphere. The only vehicles allowed are electric. Private combustion engine vehicles can only travel as far as the village of Täsch, which is about three miles away. After that, you must take a shuttle train or e-taxi into town. None of that much mattered once Longinus arrived in an Audi e-tron GT.

Bzzz.

Bzzz.

Bzzz.

Ross's cellphone rang. It was Longinus.

"I'll be there in thirty minutes," said Longinus.

Ross said, "We'll be waiting."

It was still a cold 37 degrees outside. Sporadic snow drifts covered the parking lot with remnants of melting ice. Ross was wearing his black suit with a black lambswool button-down V-neck cardigan sweater underneath, white cotton shirt, narrow black necktie, and black shoes. Lin was dressed in her bluejeans, Wimbledon white blouse, Asics sneakers, a blue sweater, and Ross's red wool jacket. Lailani gave them each a black backpack to use. They packed a change of clothes and their personal hygiene items. The backpacks were nearly identical, except Ross's contained two pistols — a 9mm Walther P-38, which Ross had taken off a dead German soldier during their 1945 time travel trip, and the Beretta model 71 in .22LR which Emanuel had given him.

Ross and Lin said their goodbyes to Lars and Lailani.

"Thank you again for helping us," said Ross as he hugged Lailani and then shook hands with Lars.

Lin said, "I can't keep track of how many times you all have come between disaster and us. Thank you, and may God always bless you."

Lars said, "You are always welcome here anytime. You are now family."

"Stay safe and return to us," said Lailani with tears in her eyes.

Then Ross heard a car horn.

Beep.

Beep.

He looked out the dining room window and saw an Audi waiting outside the front door.

Strange, he thought, *I didn't hear the car approach.*

There was no exhaust either.

Then the right side drivers door opened and out stepped a man in a long black overcoat.

It was Longinus.

His car was a new Audi e-tron GT in florett silver metallic paint. It was an electric, five-seat, grand touring automotive masterpiece. The Audi e-tron GT is an impressive high performance vehicle, with a top speed of 152 mph, and can go from zero to sixty in 2.4 seconds.

Ross and Lin walked outside and greeted Longinus.

"Lon," said Ross, offering his hand, "great to see you again."

Longinus shook his hand and said, "Greetings to you James."

Lin came up and embraced Longinus. She said, "I'm so glad you're here my friend."

Longinus looked at both of them. "We've no time to lose. We should go."

Then Longinus popped open the trunk for them to stow their bags, and unlocked the doors. Lin sat in the back, with Ross taking the left side passenger seat.

Longinus looked at his friends. "Ready?" he asked.

Ross looked back at Lin and said, "Let's go."

Longinus put the Audi in gear and took off.

"With any luck we'll be there in 3 hours," said Longinus. "I took the liberty of reserving us two rooms at the Schloss Zermatt Hotel. It's close to the Matterhorn and Nachtnebel's compound. I've got a sketch of the compound grounds in my briefcase behind the seat."

Longinus looked in the rearview mirror at Lin.

"Lin, would you pull out that sketch please," said Longinus. "It's in that briefcase on the floor back there."

Lin saw the briefcase on the floor beside her. She picked it up and placed it on her lap, then popped open the clasps. The folded sketch was lying on top of several maps.

"Here you go," said Lin handing the sketch to Ross.

Ross took the sketch and started to study it.

Longinus said, "There's something you should know about Nachtnebel."

"What's that?" asked Ross, still studying the sketch.

Longinus said, "The word 'Nachtnebel' in German literally translates to *night* and *fog,* or *foggy night.* It also was a Nazi decree issued by Hitler on December 7th 1941 targeting political activists and resistance fighters."

Ross stopped studying the sketch and looked over at Longinus.

Longinus said, "The Nachtnebel Decree victims were arrested, imprisoned, executed, or just simply disappeared. Enemies of the state were rounded up, along with their families, and gone forever."

Lin asked, "What else?"

Longinus said, "Ansgar Nachtnebel is a respected businessman, but he also dabbles in black magic. He is known as a practitioner of the dark arts, witchcraft and the occult. He's a devil worshipper. Some say he has sold his soul for his billions. If he has acquired Die Glocke, it's not for collecting. He will use it for something most evil, most heinous."

Ross and Lin just listened.

Longinus said, "Was there a man today involved with the theft of Die Glocke who was very fit, about six-foot-four, with a short gray crew cut hairstyle, and around forty years old?"

"Yeah," said Ross. "He showed me his US State Department credentials identifying himself as Special Agent Fred Kenyon."

Longinus reduced speed to go through the village of Altdorf.

"He works for Nachtnebel. His real name is Erebus Stormbrew," said Longinus. "He's former military, now a mercenary."

Now they were through the village and back on the main autobahn.

Longinus said, "Stormbrew is also an occultist, devil worshipper, and sadist. He's a practitioner of bondage, discipline, submission, and masochism, otherwise known as BDSM. His specialty is sexual torture. He loves having total power over his victims."

"Pretty sick individual," said Ross.

"Yes," said Longinus. "Definitely someone who we should plan on relieving of his existence."

Lin said, "Occult, devil worship, sadism, torture. And if they get hold of Die Glocke …"

Ross said, "They won't. We'll get it back."

Soon they were passing through the Swiss village of Münster.

Longinus said, "In less than an hour we'll be there. Why don't you two try to get some sleep?"

Lin placed the briefcase on the floor of the Audi. Then she curled up on the back seat and was soon fast asleep. Sleep came quickly for Ross too, and his dreams were filled with warring angels, demons and devils.

CHAPTER TEN

INTO ZERMATT

Zermatt Switzerland is located in the German-speaking canton of Valais. It has a population of around 6000, and is a popular skiing and mountaineering resort. Zermatt sits at an elevation of 5310 feet, and lies at the foot of the Matterhorn. Many small hamlets are situated in the valleys above Zermatt.   Most of these remain relatively uninhabited throughout the year, except for rentals by sportsmen. Billionaire Ansgar Nachtnebel owns twenty acres next to the hamlet of Furi. Many years ago he built an aerial cable car station to transport his important guests. Through his generosity, Nachtnebel offers his sky tram for tourists at certain times during the day to access the five-star restaurant he built at 1200 feet. Several times a year, Nachtnebel invites 'special' guests who share his idiosyncrasies of black magic for a weekend orgy of debauchery. Events at Epstein Island didn't hold a candle to what happened at Nachtnebel's mansion.

"We're here," said Longinus.

Ross woke up and squinted out the windshield. It was dusk and his eyes took in the picturesque town, warmly glowing, and reminiscent of something out of a Charles Dickens novel.

"Looks nice," said Ross. "Looks friendly."

Longinus said, "It is. The town is."

Longinus steered the Audi e-tron GT around the narrow streets.

"The hotel is not far from here. They serve breakfast but not dinner. I assume you two are hungry?"

Ross turned his head and looked back at Lin. She was still asleep on the back seat.

"I think I can speak for both of us, and yes, we're hungry," said Ross.

"We're famished," said Lin, opening her eyes.

Ross and Longinus laughed.

Longinus pointed with his finger. "There's a French restaurant up front here to the right."

Ross read the name off the overhead placard.

"L' Atelier Grandsire. Sounds great," said Ross.

"Very good," said Longinus. He carefully steered the Audi around to the back of the restaurant and found a place to park.

"Can you open the trunk for a second?" asked Ross. "I have something for you."

"Surely," said Longinus.

Ross followed Longinus to the rear of the Audi. Longinus pressed his key fob and popped open the trunk. Ross leaned in and unzipped his backpack. He extracted the Walther P-38 and handed it to Longinus.

"Here. You may need this. It's got eight rounds in its magazine," said Ross.

Longinus hefted the Walther in his hand and then slid it into his overcoat pocket.

"Thank you," said Longinus.

L' Atelier Grandsire Restaurant is located on Getwingstrasse. It reminds one of a quaint wooden Swiss chalet, nestled between hotels and endless snowdrifts.

The three friends exited the parking lot and walked around to the front of the restaurant. Ross held open the double-paned glass door for Lin and Longinus to enter. Longinus walked over to the maitre d' podium and said, "Guten Abend."

The maitre d' this evening was Heinz Frobe. Thirty-seven-year-old Frobe was a Swedish expat who had come to Zermatt for the skiing fifteen years ago and never left. He was six feet tall, and weighed a hundred and seventy-five athletic pounds. Frobe had piercing sky blue eyes, and kept his blonde hair cut short and combed straight back. Wearing his midnight blue Brioni tailored suit, he looked more like a young Wall Street broker than a maitre d'.

"Table for three, Mein Herr?" said Frobe.

Longinus replied, "Yes please."

Frobe picked up three menus and said, "Follow me." He led them through the crowded restaurant to a rear table by the fireplace. He pulled out and held a chair for Lin to sit down. "I'll send your waitress Nina right over," he said.

The three friends looked over the menu.

A blonde waitress scurried over to the table.

"May I take your order please?" she said.

Nineteen-year-old Nina Abderhalden had been a waitress at L' Atelier Grandsire Restaurant for the past six months. Nina was a native of Zermatt, and was working as a waitress to pay for her exercise science degree from the University of Zurich. Tonight she was wearing a burgundy L'Agence stretch-leather bodycon midi dress. The dress had open collar and shoulders, with a gothic baroque corset bodice and shirred waist ruffle hem. The dress was tight across her breasts and low in the back. It was cinched to her waist by a two-inch-wide leather belt with gold baroque buckle. Her feet were nestled in three-inch-heeled black baroque shoes resplendent with matching black baroque bows. Her blonde hair was cut in a sassy French bob with bangs reaching to her eyebrows. Her beautiful youthful face was reminiscent of a young Barbara Eden. Nina wore ruby lipstick with a wet gloss to accent her sensuous mouth. Her fingernails were cut short and painted gloss eruption green. She smelled of Miss Dior eau de parfum. Nina radiated a healthy, fun-loving, joyful ambience.

Longinus said, "Ladies first," and nodded to Lin.

Lin put the menu down and looked at Ross. "What do you think Jamie?"

Ross had asked the next question at dozens of restaurants around the world. He enjoyed the routine and loved the responses. Mostly though, he loved the soup.

"Do you have French onion soup today?" inquired Ross.

Nina looked up from her notepad.

She thought to herself, *This guy's in for a treat.*

"Yes sir. The very best French onion soup in the whole of Switzerland," she said proudly.

"Okay," said Ross. "I'll have French onion soup, with a large thin slice of cheese melted over the top. And I would like the bacon wrapped filet, medium, with green beans, and a salad with thousand island dressing. And bring me a Eichhof beer please, along with a water."

Nina smiled and looked at Lin, raising her eyebrows. "And for you Madame?"

"Give me all the same," said Lin smiling.

Nina wrote it down and looked at Longinus.

"I'll also have the same, except put Italian dressing on my salad please," said Longinus.

Ross gathered the menus and handed them to Nina.

Longinus reached inside his suit coat pocket and pulled out his Muratti Ambassador brand cigarettes.

"Do you mind if I smoke?" he asked.

Ross and Lin shook their heads.

Longinus tapped the packet with the crook of his left forefinger and extracted one. Ross immediately pulled out his Zippo lighter and stretched his arm across the table. He popped open the top and flicked the thumbwheel downward, igniting a wavering bluish flame.

Longinus eyed Ross and leaned his face in to permit Ross to light his Muratti. He cocked his head to the side and allowed himself the luxury of a long, slow draw. The Centurian held the smoke in his lungs for a moment, and then tilted his head upwards hissing the tobacco vapors out through his nostrils in the direction of the fireplace.

"Thank you," said Longinus.

Lin said, "You do know that those will kill you?"

Longinus changed the subject.

"James," he said, "this Nachtnebel is a very wicked man. He topples economies without a second thought. He takes great pleasure in destroying people. Women are enticed to his parties and disappear completely."

Lin asked, "Is he trafficking them?"

"In a way," said Longinus. "He sexually abuses them in his satanic rituals. He breaks them down."

Longinus stubbed out his cigarette in the ashtray.

"He breaks them into pieces."

Just then Nina returned with a tray of food. She placed the soups and steaks in front of them, along with the drinks.

"Be careful, the plates are very hot," gushed Nina.

"Thank you," said Ross.

As Nina left, Longinus said, "I'm looking forward to this soup. I've always been mystified by your fascination with French onion soup."

Ross picked up his knife and fork to cut his steak when Lin quietly tapped him on his arm.

Longinus had bowed his head in silent prayer.

Heavenly Father, allow me to help this young couple in their quest. Deliver us from the evil one, and protect us in battle. In the name of your holy son Jesus, I ask this, amen.

Ross gently put down his utensils, and he and Lin bowed their heads.

Longinus looked up, and then the three friends turned their concentration to their dinners.

CHAPTER ELEVEN

DIABOLISTS

During dinner, Longinus filled Ross and Lin in on the activities of Ansgar Nachtnebel.

"He earned his billions by selling currencies short in foreign countries. The man pits countries against each other and crashes economies. Even during the war as a child he grew quite a reputation for himself by aiding his father turn in the locations of suspected Jews to the Nazi SS."

Ross and Lin just listened.

Longinus said, "Today he is a ninety-one-year-old gentleman, only he is no gentleman. He still manipulates currencies, only now he is immersed in politics. He funds left-wing communist judges and attorney generals who support radical progressive ideas. Nachtnebel is responsible for thousands of criminals being freed under 'no cash bail' reforms. He is currently trying to destabilize the economies of the United States, Israel, and Great Britain."

Ross said, "What about this satanism thing?"

Longinus said, "Nachtnebel started practicing devil worship in the 1960s. He seeks to gain money and power anyway he can, even if it is through dark pacts with evil spirits. Every so often Nachtnebel sends out invitations to his like-minded friends and they gather at his mansion here. They call themselves Diabolists. They perform a black mass, which is usually filled up with a bunch of mumbo-jumbo and sex. They take turns raping a victim, normally a female. She is usually kidnapped, stripped naked, tied between an 'X' wooden frame, and then sexually abused. The finale takes place when a bed is brought before the altar with black sheets and black pillows. The victim is laid on the bed and it becomes a free-for-all orgy. It all amounts to gang rape and a BDSM freak show."

"And this guy probably has Die Glocke?" asked Lin.

Longinus said, "He does have it. I have a friend at Sion airport, the closest airport to Zermatt. A private cargo plane came in this afternoon owned by Nachtnebel. The manifest says it was carrying antiques. It was unloaded and taken to Nachtnebel's private hangar where he keeps his vintage planes. My friend took this picture on his cellphone while they were unloading it."

Longinus pulled out his cellphone and showed Ross and Lin the image. It was half covered with the gray tarp, but there was no doubt it was Die Glocke.

Longinus said, "Nachtnebel collects expensive antiques from all over the world. His mansion is like a museum."

"So," said Ross, "we're going to have to get into his place."

Longinus caught hold of Nina's eye and motioned her over.

"Please bring us three mint teas," said Longinus.

Nina nodded her head and soon was back placing three steaming cups of alpine mint tea on their table.

Lin picked up her tea and asked, "How are we going to get into Nachtnebel's mansion?"

Longinus took a sip of his tea and said, "Through a tunnel. You see, Nachtnebel owns a restaurant on the mountain at 1200 feet. Tourists have to take a cable car sky tram to access it. The tunnel was built by Nachtnebel as his private entrance. It runs from the restaurant to his home."

Ross took a sip of his tea and looked at Longinus and Lin.

"That's the plan then. Tomorrow. And I doubt if Nachtnebel or anyone else will be able to do anything with Die Glocke before then," said Ross.

"Why do you say that?" asked Lin.

"Because," said Ross, as he reached into his suit coat pocket and pulled out some folded papers, "it would be awful hard to operate Die Glocke without the instructions."

Nina brought the check and Ross paid it with his credit card. Then Longinus suggested they head over to the hotel. The Schloss Zermatt Hotel was located at number 18 Bahnhofplatz. It was close to the train station, restaurants, and shopping. It was also close to the cable car station. Longinus had arranged for two rooms across the hall from each other on the second floor.

"Shall we meet at seven o'clock tomorrow morning?" asked Longinus.

"Yeah," said Ross. "At the restaurant downstairs for breakfast."

"See you then," said Longinus. He entered his room and closed the door.

Ross slipped the electronic coded plastic card key into its slot. The small door lock light turned from red to green with an audible *click.* Pulling the card out, Ross held the door open for Lin. Once inside he locked the door shut.

"What time is it Lin?" asked Ross.

Lin looked at her Citizen Eco-drive ProMaster watch. "It's eight-thirty."

"How do you feel?" asked Ross.

Lin said, "Totally exhausted."

"Me too," said Ross. "I didn't get much sleep in the car."

Lin said, "I think I'll just take a shower and then go to bed."

"Okay," said Ross. "I'll take mine after you're done."

Lin stripped off her clothes in front of Ross. She carefully folded them and placed them inside the top dresser drawer. Then she walked nude into the bathroom and shut the door behind her.

Ross removed his pistol from the backpack. He slightly pulled back the slide of the Beretta 71 to make sure a round was chambered, and then placed the pistol on the nightstand by his side of the bed. He opened the lower drawer in the dresser and put inside his backpack. Then he placed Lin's backpack inside the top drawer next to her clothes. Ross took off all his clothes and hung them up in the closet. He took particular care in trying to make sure that his suit coat and pants remained relatively wrinkle-free. Then he brushed his teeth in the small kitchenette sink.

The large queen-sized bed looked enticing, and Ross slid his nude body in between its crisp clean sheets. As soon as his head hit the pillow he was fast asleep.

Lin finished her shower and stepped out of the bathroom while toweling herself off.

"I'm all finished," said Lin, "your turn …"

Then she saw Ross sound asleep.

She crept over on her tippy toes and gently kissed him on the cheek.

Lin whispered, "Goodnight my prince."

CHAPTER TWELVE

URGENT CALL

Ross awoke with the jolt of an electric spark. It was ten minutes before six o'clock in the morning. As usual, he had mentally impelled himself to wake up through sheer force of his will.

So as not to wake Lin, he silently staggered into the bathroom, flicking on the lights. He turned on the shower and stepped in, not wasting any time. In three minutes his shower was over. Ross stepped out of the shower stall and wrapped one of the white terrycloth hotel towels around his waist.

Wiping his right hand across the steam covered mirror, he looked at himself. He shaved quickly, then lowered his head towards the sink and splashed hot water across his face to rinse off the remaining residue. Then he crept quietly back into the bedroom and slid back into bed between the sheets.

Bzzz.

Bzzzz.

Bzzzzz.

Ross picked up his cellphone from the nightstand. Squinting at it, he saw that it was General Matthews calling. He swung his legs out of the bed, stood up, and quietly walked into the bathroom.

What the hell am I'm going to tell him? thought Ross. *What can I say? That Die Glocke was stolen by fraudulent State Department guys and now I'm in Zermatt Switzerland about to amount an assault on a billionaire's mountain fortress?*

Ross decided not to answer it, and to let the phone go to message. He placed his phone back on the nightstand. Then he turned his head and looked at Lin.

Lin had rolled over onto her back. She stretched both of her arms up towards the headboard. The covers had fallen down to just below her navel. The softness of her skin was in direct contrast to the hardness of her erect nipples pointing upwards.

Lin's nude body teased at him.

Ross was immediately reminded of the beautiful *Sleeping Bather* nineteenth century painting by Pierre-Auguste Renoir. He had studied the great painters in an electives art course years ago while attending Texas Christian University.

He couldn't help but smile.

My God, she's beautiful.

She's all I want in this life.

I wish this moment would last forever.

But Ross knew he had a mission to do.

He had to get on it.

The mission can wait five minutes, he thought.

Ross leaned over and gently kissed Lin on her soft lips.

Her scent intoxicated him.

His chest brushed across her nipples, further adding fuel to his already consuming desire.

"Good morning, Lin."

Lin smiled and her eyelids fluttered open.

"Good morning, handsome."

Lin reached out and wrapped her arms around Ross's neck.

She pulled him close and kissed him wantonly on the lips.

Ross's defenses waned and he fell under her magical spell.

Lin's luxuriously sensuous body folded together perfectly with Ross's muscle-hardened torso. She smiled and played with Ross's hair for a few seconds, twisting and turning it in her fingers. She tried to brush it off his forehead, but it just fell back down again only in more disarray. She slowly rolled over on top of Ross's body. Ross stiffened, and Lin arched her back and rocked her hips, grasping Ross's chest with both of her hands. She thrust back and forth, and gyrated her hips again and again, over and over, until she suddenly fell forward on top of Ross's chest.

Now she blossomed around Ross and opened herself fully to him, while pressing back on Ross's chest with both of her hands.

Lin smiled at Ross and allowed him to envelope her —

— to overcome her —

— to seduce her —

— to love her.

Lin held on tight as Ross kissed her long —

— and slow —

— and tenderly.

Then Lin closed her eyes and clutched Ross, hoping the moment would never end.

Their movements flowed like a powerful current in the sea, ever smoothly and increasing, until the undulations of the swell crested and crashed into the shore in all its majesty.

Then the hotel courtesy deskphone rang.

Brriing.

Brriinngg.

Ross picked up the telephone receiver.

"Hello?" he said.

"Good morning sir. This is your courtesy wake-up call."

Ross answered automatically, "Thank you," and then hung up the receiver.

"It's time to get ready to meet Lon," said Ross.

Lin jumped out of bed and hurried to the bathroom.

"I'll just be a minute," she said over her shoulder.

Ross and Lin took the elevator down to the lobby. Ross immediately noticed Longinus sitting in one of the lounge chairs reading the local newspaper.

"Good morning Lon," said Ross.

Longinus said, "Good morning. Did you sleep well?"

"Oh," said Lin stretching her arms, "I slept like a baby."

Ross said, "Let's grab some breakfast."

The three friends walked through the lobby to the restaurant.

"Guten Morgen," said Hans the restaurant host.

Ross replied with, "Guten Morgen. May we have a table for three please?"

"Certainly," said Hans. "Please follow me."

Hans led them through the crowded restaurant to a side table.

"I'll send your waiter right over," said Hans, and he placed three menus on their table.

Ross pulled out a chair for Lin to sit down.

"This looks like a great place," said Ross.

Longinus took a seat and looked at the menu. "I've never been much for breakfast," he said. "What do you recommend?"

Ross took a second to look at the menu.

"You can't go wrong with steak and eggs," said Ross as he continued scanning the menu. "They also have potato pancakes. That's instead of hash browns. You gotta have a couple of those."

Longinus said, "What's a potato pancake?"

Ross said, "It's made from grated potatoes and onions, with a little flour, salt and pepper. You mash it flat like a burger or a pancake."

"Okay," said Longinus. "What kind of steak do you get for breakfast?"

Ross said, "Usually it can be either a New York strip, a ribeye, or even a flat iron steak."

Lin said, "I'm going to just have yogurt and some toast with jelly. I'm still stuffed from last night."

A young waiter arrived and placed three waters on their table.

"Good morning. My name is Niklaus. May I take your order?"

While Niklaus was writing down their order, across the room at a table sat someone observing the entire scene — Erebus Stormbrew.

Stormbrew had taken a break from Nachtnebel's mansion and rode the cable car down to Zermatt for breakfast. It was just coincidence that he happened into the Schloss Zermatt Hotel for breakfast.

They don't see me, thought Stormbrew. *That's definitely Captain Ross and the girl. That other man must be a colleague.*

Stormbrew finished his coffee and looked at his check. He placed thirty Swiss francs on the table and stood up to leave, being careful to be inconspicuous.

Once outside, Stormbrew raised his collar to the blustery cold weather. He thrust his hands into the pockets of his overcoat and walked briskly to the sky tram station.

Ross and his colleagues are here for Die Glocke, he thought. *Somehow he knows that Nachtnebel has it. And tonight is one of Nachtnebel's satanic parties. He'll have twenty or thirty guests there celebrating a black mass. After that ceremony, the group will descend into a wild orgy.*

A debauched smile crept across his face.

The orgy will end with the degradation and rape of a young woman.

Stormbrew arrived at the sky tram station. He removed the plastic pass card which was on a cord around his neck and showed it to the attendant.

The attendant took Stormbrew's pass card and put it through a scanner. The scanner showed that Erebus Stormbrew was a very important employee of Herr Ansgar Nachtnebel.

The attendant returned the pass card and said, "Here you are Herr Stormbrew. Please give Herr Nachtnebel my best wishes."

Stormbrew took his pass card and found a seat on the sky tram. The huge gears started to move and the cables became taught, and the cable car started to ascend almost noiselessly.

Stormbrew thought to himself, *Nachtnebel told me he was giving me the girl tonight as a special treat, whoever she is. I'm going to make sure it's Lin Sparrow.*

CHAPTER THIRTEEN

TREACHERY

Longinus paid for the breakfast, and the three friends made their way to the sky tram station. The station consisted of an operations building with a small concessions stand and cashier where you could purchase your tickets. The building also housed the electric motor and control monitors. The sky tram was composed of two stationary steel cables for support, and a third moving cable for propulsion. The gondola itself could accommodate up to twenty people.

Ross walked up to the window and purchased three round trip tickets.

"Here you are sir," said the young blonde woman behind the acrylic window. "Enjoy your trip."

Ross said, "Thank you."

There were about a dozen other people riding in the gondola with them. Ross wondered who was there for breakfast, who was there for sightseeing, and who was there for one of Nachtnebel's parties?

The gears meshed and the gondola lifted upwards with a slight swing and a jolt. The three friends fixed their gaze through the windows on the frozen wintry countryside beneath them. The view was simply magnificent with the Matterhorn standing like a protective angel overlooking the tiny vulnerable village of Zermatt. The snow-capped peaks loomed menacingly and the snow-laden valleys were littered with skiers speeding down their groomed pistes or ski runs.

"Impressive," said Ross pointing with his finger.

Lin said, "It is very beautiful. What do you think Lon?"

Longinus kept looking towards Nachtnebel's restaurant on the mountain. "Yes," he said, "impressive."

It took about fifteen minutes for the sky tram to reach the restaurant on the summit. It slid into its docking station and came to an abrupt stop. The tram attendant opened the sliding doors and everyone disembarked.

Nachtnebel's restaurant was ironically named *Devil's Corner.* Some would say it was named after the dangerous advanced ski run which bore that name and could be observed from its panoramic windows. Others whispered it got its name from the strange goings-on at the eccentric billionaires' mansion. Either way, tourists flocked to eat there.

Ross, Lin, and Longinus stood for a while on the outside observation deck overlooking the valley.

Ross said, "Tell me about the restaurant tunnel."

"It runs from the restaurant to Nachtnebel's mansion," said Longinus. "There's an entrance through the back of the restaurant. Inside the tunnel is a Bergbahn."

"What's that?" asked Ross.

Longinus said, "It's an underground rail system. As an American, I guess you would call it a subway. It's pretty simple really. Nachtnebel uses it to transport his guests to and from the restaurant. You just press a button to order it, like you would order an elevator."

Ansgar Nachtnebel and Erebus Stormbrew walked into the library. The room held a vast collection of treasures, from Egyptian art to Mesopotamian artifacts. The walls were adorned with paintings from Picasso, Degas, and Matisse. The library housed first editions of Hemingway, Steinbeck, Fleming, Cervantes, Dostoevsky and Hugo. The two men sat down in plush red leather-bound chairs next to the grand fireplace. Stormbrew clicked a remote and a huge monitor above the fireplace came to life. He scrolled through various camera views then settled on one in particular. It was a live feed image at the Devil's Corner Restaurant.

"There you are sir," said Stormbrew.

Nachtnebel sat forward in his chair. He stared at the image intensely. "Yes, yes I see. It is him. It is Captain James Ross."

Stormbrew said, "Yes sir. Since we last spoke, I've received an update from our Chinese friends on the other two individuals."

Stormbrew pressed the zoom button on the remote control and brought it to focus on Lin Sparrow's face.

"The girl is a Miss Lin Sparrow. She's most probably the girlfriend of Captain Ross."

Stormbrew next zoomed in on the face of Longinus.

"The man next to her is one Lon G. Inus," said Stormbrew.

"Lon G. Inus?" said Nachtnebel. "Who's he?"

Stormbrew said, "That's a little harder. All our queries through Interpol and the Kantonspolizei have proved negative. Even our Chinese friends don't know much about him, except that Mister Inus is suspected of having helped Ross and Lin Sparrow in their mission to stop the theft of the Spear of Destiny."

Nachtnebel thought back to his good friend and colleague Wu Qiang who was killed just last week.

"And were these three responsible for the death of Doctor Wu Qiang?" asked Nachtnebel.

Stormbrew said, "Most assuredly sir."

Just then a knock came on the library doors.

"Enter," said Nachtnebel.

It was Aemilius Urs, Nachtnebel's trusted manservant.

"Would you care for a drink, sir?" asked Aemilius.

Ansgar turned around and said, "Yes, yes I would. Bring me an Armagnac brandy. And bring one for Erebus."

Aemilius bowed. "Very good sir."

Then he scurried off to fetch the brandy.

Nachtnebel said, "I've always preferred Pyrenees brandy as opposed to the northern. Just the right amount of sweetness in the grapes."

Stormbrew really didn't know what the man was talking about, but he answered, "So do I."

Aemilius returned with the brandy and poured them each a glass.

"Is there anything else I can do for you, sir?" asked Aemilius.

Nachtnebel said, "No, that'll be all. Thank you."

Aemilius walked out of the library and closed the doors behind him.

Nachtnebel reclined back in his chair and said, "I want you to take care of this Mister Lon Inus. And I want you to bring James Ross before me."

Stormbrew nodded his head.

"And what about the girl?" he asked.

Nachtnebel said, "She'll make a fine subject for our little gathering tonight. You can have her at the end. I want Ross to watch everything that happens to her. Just be sure you finish them both."

Stormbrew wet his lips.

"It will be my pleasure, sir."

CHAPTER FOURTEEN

GUESTS ARRIVE

Nachtnebel's guests were flying in from around the world. There was much preparation for the celebration tonight. His staff was working overtime. Of course the mass itself would occur at midnight, but before that there would be a huge feast at around eight o'clock, followed by a tour of the mansion, and, as a special treat, a tour of his latest acquisition — Die Glocke. Nachtnebel planned on incorporating Die Glocke into the ceremony. He would have loved to provide a practical demonstration of the device's operational capabilities, and currently had his researchers combing through archive documents of the Third Reich's Ministry of Science and Technology to try and find instructions on how to operate it. The local Kantonspolizei were aware of Nachtnebel's exotic tastes, and with monetary contributions could easily be bribed to look the other way for an evening. Several times in the past the evening's female sacrifice succumbed to abuse, so Nachtnebel had his personal physician prepare the death certificates.

The guests were usually divided into two groups. One group actually believed in satanism and black magic. This group practiced the rituals and believed in the spells and incantations. They thought the world could be manipulated to their will through black magic. The second group were converts nonetheless, however, mostly they considered the occult as a bunch of mumbo-jumbo and were in it for the thrills.

It was implied that Nachtnebel had given Stormbrew a certain amount of control over his security staff of eight men, including his Chief of Information Technology Deiter Moss. Moss was kept busy monitoring the live video feed of Ross and his friends.

"And they just arrived at the Devil's Corner Restaurant?" asked Stormbrew.

"Yes, Herr Stormbrew," said Moss. "It appears they are ordering coffee and socializing."

Stormbrew said, "Let me take a look." He sat down next to Moss and peered into the monitor. He saw Ross and Lin sitting on one side of a table with Inus on the other side. They appeared as if they were tourists just enjoying the morning.

"Yes, I see," said Stormbrew. "Keep an eye on them for me. Let me know the second anything unusual happens."

Moss said, "As you wish, Herr Stormbrew."

Stormbrew excused himself and walked out of the IT room. He pulled out his cellphone and texted to Nachtnebel: *Sir, I need to talk to you. Are you available?*

In a few seconds Nachtnebel responded with a text: *Yes. Come down to the hangar.*

The hangar encompassed over five acres, and it attached to the six-story mansion on the main level. It reminded one of a very large garage or warehouse. The hangar housed Nachtnebel's largest collectibles including his vintage automobile collection, his vintage airplane collection, and now his latest acquisition — Die Glocke.

Unfolding down in Zermatt at the concierge desk of the Schloss Hotel was a most unusual confrontation. The concierge guest relations manager today was Arnim Schmid. Schmid was thirty-five years old, with blonde hair and sapphire blue eyes. He was a native Swiss-born son of a prominent business family. Some considered his personality to be one of arrogance, but Schmid chalked himself up to just being efficient, professional, and no-nonsense.

"I have told you sir, we at the Schloss Zermatt do not give out that kind of information," said Schmid.

Clive Maxsted was visibly irritated. He was not used to people stonewalling him. Maxsted was a career Foreign Service Officer (FSO) with the US State Department. He had been sent, along with two Diplomatic Security Service (DSS) agents, to secure Die Glocke and facilitate its return to the United States. Maxsted in particular had been chosen because it was thought he had experience with Captain James Ross — positive experience. But Maxsted secretly hated Ross. He had tried to arrest Ross in the Philippines for a Neutrality Act violation last year while Ross was rescuing a CIA friend, and last week in Vienna Maxsted tried to arrest Ross yet again while searching for Die Glocke. Maxsted loathed the military and especially Special Forces men. He considered SF men to be overrated and egotistical.

Ross stretches the rules and has no regard for authority. He thinks he is untouchable because of that green beret he wears. If Ross is holding back information about Die Glocke I'll find out, thought Maxsted.

The Diplomatic Security Service (DSS) is the security branch of the US Department of State. It conducts criminal investigations, threat analysis, cybersecurity, counterterrorism, counterintelligence, and personal protection of people, property, and information for the US State Department. Consisting of approximately 2500 special agents, the DSS is tasked with protecting visiting foreign dignitaries and US diplomatic missions abroad. Today, a DSS team from the US Embassy in Bern was dispatched to recover the mythical World War Two Nazi time machine known as *the Bell* and codenamed *Die Glocke*. The team consisted of two special agents, and one FSO, Clive Maxsted.

"Look," said Maxsted, "all I want to know is if Mister James Ross is registered at this hotel. That's all."

Schmid said, "Oh, well when you put it that way, the answer is still no."

Maxsted almost blew up. He pulled out his State Department credentials and flipped open the billfold to impress the Concierge.

Schmid leaned forward across the counter and peered at the credentials.

"Yes sir, I see you are Mister Clive Maxsted. I'm pleased to meet you," said Schmid. Then he tapped on the name tag on his vest. "And here's my name, and the Schloss Zermatt Hotel does not give out personal information to anyone on a confidential basis, unless of course it is an official police sanctioned matter."

Maxsted became visibly frustrated.

Schmid said, "And sir, I don't see anything on your credentials saying that you are a member of the police."

"All right," said Maxsted exasperated. "I'll return with your local police. Will that make you happy?"

Schmid kept his cool. "I'm sure you can appreciate that we just don't give out any information of anyone, whether they are guests or not. The Schloss Zermatt Hotel operates under the epitome of the utmost discretion in these matters."

Maxsted frowned and said, "Uh-huh, sure."

PART THREE

The day of which we fear as our last is but the birthday of eternity.

Lucius Annaeus Seneca
4 BC — 65 AD
Roman Stoic Philosopher

CHAPTER FIFTEEN

MASTER PLAN

Stormbrew walked into the vastness of the hangar with his footsteps echoing off the walls. His eyes took in the sheer opulence of the vintage airplanes and automobiles which were part of Nachtnebel's collection. There was a black and gold 1937 Rolls-Royce Phantom III, a midnight blue 1929 Audi Zwickau 20/100 Type SS, a racing green 1939 Bentley 4 1/4 liter sport coupe, and an oyster white 1931 Mercedes-Benz SSK roadster. The airplanes consisted of a 1943 Focke-Wulf Fw 190 fighter, a 1935 Junkers Ju-52 transport, a 1944 Horten Ho 229 jet flying wing in working condition, and a 1938 Boeing 314 Pan Am Clipper. The Boeing was nicknamed "the flying boat" because it was designed to take off and land on water. Also inside the hangar were two forklifts, a Mercedes-Benz flatbed truck, and a Mercedes-Benz Arocs 3-axle tractor with heavy lift loading crane. And in the center of it, in all its grandeur, sat the Nazi time machine known as Die Glocke.

Very impressive, thought Stormbrew. *You could start a war with this.*

Nachtnebel was standing and peering into a large display case with various World War II weapons and armaments.

"Herr Nachtnebel," said Stormbrew, "can we talk?"

Nachtnebel turned and said, "But of course Erebus. What's on your mind?"

There was a bar complete with barman set up next to the display case. Nachtnebel sat down in one of the huge red leather upholstered lounge chairs and motioned for Stormbrew to come over.

"Join me," said Nachtnebel.

Stormbrew walked over and took a seat next to his employer.

"May I offer you a drink?" asked Nachtnebel.

Stormbrew said, "Just some coffee, please."

Nachtnebel turned to the barman and said, "Two coffees. And add a little honey in mine."

The barman brought the coffees over and placed them on the small oak table between the two men. Then he hurried back to the bar and busied himself.

Nachtnebel said, "What's troubling you, Erebus?"

Stormbrew smiled and replied, "Nothing is troubling me sir, only I wanted to know the time frame for this evening? And I wanted to know how fast you want my men to secure Ross and his party?"

Nachtnebel sipped his coffee and said, "Yes, well, many of my guests are still arriving. They won't all be here until late this afternoon. We plan on dinner around six, and then cocktails."

Stormbrew sipped his coffee and listened to the old man.

"The ceremony will start at midnight, assuming all goes well with bringing the girl here. Do you anticipate any issues?"

Stormbrew said, "I could grab them now. They are having coffee at the restaurant. As far as issues go, I assume Ross will be armed?" He raised an eyebrow to his boss in query.

Nachtnebel said, "Most assuredly. Probably all three of them." Then he motioned with his head. "You know they are here for Die Glocke, don't you?"

Stormbrew said, "Yes Mein Herr."

"Ross thinks he can swoop in here and take it back to his red-white-and-blue benefactors," said Nachtnebel. "You know, Ross saved my life during the war."

Stormbrew relaxed back in his chair and sipped his coffee.

Nachtnebel's eyes became glassy.

"The war was almost over. It was during the battle of Berlin — 20 April 1945 — the Soviet siege. The Russians were swarming through the city. Fighting was house-to-house. They were savages. They killed all the men, and raped the women, girls, and the boys. It didn't matter to them. The Russians were brutal, vicious, cruel savages. That's where I lost my faith in God. My father was a soldier. I don't even know what happened to him. When Hitler started losing the war, they just came and took the old men to be soldiers. That was it. No choice. The Russians took my mother. I never saw her again. But I saw what happened to my sister. My little sister was taken and raped by three Russians." Nachtnebel was lost in time. "You can't imagine the horror. They tore her to pieces and killed her. I ran away so fast. I hid in a garbage heap. Then I was swept up into the Wehrmacht."

Nachtnebel took another sip of his coffee.

"Well, what was left of the Wehrmacht anyway. I was eleven then. A proud member of the 3rd SS Panzer Division Totenkopf. I had been awarded the Iron Cross. But even before that, I was a member of the Hitler Youth. I was proud of Germany. I was proud of how Hitler had lifted us from our knees to a position of strength. As a child, I accompanied my father to help the Nazis confiscate the belongings of Jews. We were told that all Germany's ills could be blamed on our Jewish population." Nachtnebel shook his head. "There was nothing to do, except to survive. Survive anyway you can. One had to survive."

Stormbrew said, "Incredible."

Nachtnebel looked at Stormbrew and smiled.

"I have a watch in my trophy case in the library. It's a Benrus. It was given to me by a soldier during the Russian siege of Berlin. There's nothing unusual about that. Benrus has been making watches since 1921. But this watch is special. It has a manufacture date on the back. The date is November 2020."

Stormbrew finished his coffee and put down his cup.

"But how is that possible?" Stormbrew asked.

"Because," said Nachtnebel, "the man who gave it to me in 1945 was Captain James Ross. He had used Die Glocke to travel back in time, and somehow ended up at the precise moment I needed a savior."

Stormbrew said, "But how do you know it was Ross?"

"Because I saw him," said Nachtnebel. "He saved my life. One doesn't soon forget someone who saved his life during war. And I have a dossier on him from our Chinese friends. Every picture of Ross shows him wearing the Benrus — the exact same Benrus he gave me on 20 April 1945. There is only one way Ross could have done that."

"How's that?" asked Stormbrew.

"By using Die Glocke to travel back in time," replied Nachtnebel.

Stormbrew leaned back and folded his arms across his chest.

"Mein Herr, if Ross is your savior, why kill him?" said Stormbrew.

Nachtnebel said, "Because Ross killed my very good friend Doctor Wu Qiang. I met him years ago at the World Psychotherapy Forum in Geneva. I was giving a lecture on 'Quantum Millionaire Theory' which Doctor Qiang attended. He believed mankind was in need of a reboot. So did I. As we got to know each other better, we decided that what was needed was to get China and the United States to outspend each other through war. Someone who could speculate on such an event and the resultant armaments build up would make billions. Everything was coming together last week at the Trump/Xi Vienna summit. You see, all we needed was a patsy to assassinate those two heads of state. Once that was done, China and America would blame each other and war would break out. It would be revealed that the patsy had been brainwashed by the Chinese, and the rest as they say, would be history. And guess who the patsy turned out to be?"

Stormbrew shook his head.

Nachtnebel said, "The patsy turned out to be Captain James Ross. It was incredible happenstance. And Ross and his friends murdered my friend Wu, and he got away with Die Glocke. So you see, Ross must pay with his life."

Stormbrew finally understood. The pieces of the complex puzzle had come together.

"So," said Stormbrew, "I'll kill this Inus guy. And as far as James Ross and Lin Sparrow …"

Nachtnebel said, "I want you to bring James Ross before me."

Stormbrew nodded his head.

"And the girl?" he asked.

Nachtnebel said, "I want Ross to watch everything that happens tonight. I want Ross to feel the loss of what he loves most. She'll make a fine sacrifice to Lucifer. You can have her at the end. Just be sure you finish them both."

Stormbrew said, "Consider it done, Mein Herr."

CHAPTER SIXTEEN

DEVIL'S CORNER

The waitress brought a pot of steaming coffee and a basket of Bürli bread with strawberry jam to their table. Her name was Ingrid Meier. Ingrid worked at the Devil's Corner Restaurant only part time. Her other job was as a tour guide at the Jaegerhof Hotel. Ingrid was twenty-one years old, shoulder length blonde hair parted in the middle, with cobalt blue eyes, and looked like a young Elke Sommer. She was dressed in a traditional black Dirndl, thigh length, complete with large bow on her left hip, and white corset straps laced up and across her bosom. Her feet were nestled in three-inch black pumps by Alfani.

After her second cup, Lin said, "Excuse me gentlemen, but this coffee is going right through me." Then she got up to go to the ladies' room.

Ross and Longinus momentarily stood while Lin excused herself.

From where Ross was seated, he had a clear view of the entire Devil's Corner Restaurant.

"I see the entrance to the subway," said Ross. "It's right next to the panoramic windows behind you. It's clearly marked."

Longinus turned around and looked.

"Yes. The only issue will be us actually taking the Bergbahn, ah, I mean subway, since it goes directly to Nachtnebel's private residence," said Longinus.

"Yeah," said Ross, "and I don't think we're on any invitation list."

Longinus said, "We'll have to think up an excuse."

"Or," said Ross, "create a diversion."

"Excellent," said Longinus. "What do you have in mind?"

Ross thought for a second.

"A restroom fires usually works well," said Ross.

Longinus nodded his head.

"Very well," said Longinus. "When the staff is busy with the fire, we'll activate the subway."

Ross said, "And we can always tell them we thought it was an emergency exit."

Ross lifted his left hand to look at the time, but then remembered he didn't have his Benrus anymore.

Lin's taking a long time in the restroom, thought Ross.

Longinus saw the look of worry creep across Ross's face.

"Is something the matter James?" asked Longinus.

Ross said, "Lin's been gone a while."

Longinus looked at the 1940 Eterna chronograph watch on his left wrist.

"It's ten-forty-five," Longinus said. "I believe she's been gone around fifteen minutes."

Ross raised his arm and caught the attention of Ingrid their waitress.

Ingrid walked over to the table and said, "More coffee sir?"

Ross said, "No thank you, but can you please check the ladies' room and see if our friend is all right?"

"Certainly," said Ingrid.

"Her name is Lin," said Ross.

Ross's eyes followed Ingrid as she walked back to the ladies' room and went inside. She came out after a few minutes and walked back to their table shaking her head.

"I'm sorry," said Ingrid, "but no one is in there."

Ross immediately jumped up knocking over his chair and rushed to the ladies' room. He threw open the door and walked inside. Ross checked every stall. Lin was nowhere to be found.

"My goodness," said Ingrid looking at Longinus. "Maybe they had a fight? Maybe she took the sky tram back to town?"

Longinus picked up Ross's chair and then sat back down.

Ross walked back to the table and stood there staring at Longinus.

"Lin's gone," he said. "She's gone."

Ross grabbed hold of Ingrid's hand.

Longinus said, "Easy, James."

"Tell me, Ingrid," said Ross, "is there another way out of the restroom?"

Ingrid became frightened. She looked into Ross's eyes and saw that this was no man to play with.

"Um, yes, yes there is," said Ingrid. "It's through the utility closet. It opens into the walkway to the Bergbahn."

Ross released his grip on Ingrid's hand and looked at Longinus.

Ingrid said, "They only use it to take out the garbage."

Ross reached in his pants pocket and pulled out a hundred Swiss franc note and dropped it on the table. Then he and Longinus hurried to the ladies' room. Ingrid was about to raise her arm and yell at Ross to stop, but thought better of it.

"Americans," she said to herself while shaking her head.

Ross grabbed the handle and wretched the restroom door open. Once inside, he saw the utility closet and opened its door. He was greeted by mops, brooms, and buckets. Then he saw the exit door. It had an envelope taped to it with his name on it.

Christ, thought Ross.

Ross pulled off the envelope and opened it. Inside was a note addressed to him. It read:

Captain Ross: Your friend has graciously accepted my invitation to our party tonight. It starts at midnight. You are invited.

Longinus saw Ross reading the note.

"What is it?" asked Longinus.

Ross said, "They've got Lin. Somehow, someway, they've got Lin."

Ross opened the exit door, and he and Longinus stepped through. The outside chill of wet snow flurries hit their faces. Then he handed Longinus the note. Ross scanned the area and saw nothing, then he looked at the ground and squatted down. The snow was disturbed with definite signs of someone being dragged through it.

"Look at that," said Ross as he pointed to the disrupted snow.

Longinus bent down and scanned the scene. He saw the signs of the struggle. It appeared as if they dragged Lin on to the subway.

Ross and Longinus stood up. Their breath was coming out in puffs circling and disappearing skyward.

Ross said, "It's got to be Nachtnebel. He's the reason beautiful young women disappear from around here, for his rituals, for his ceremonies. It's got to be him. He's asking me to come. He's begging me."

Longinus said, "I agree. So what do you want to do?"

Ross felt for the reassuring steel of the Beretta 71 in his suit coat pocket.

"Something massive," said Ross. "Something massive."

CHAPTER SEVENTEEN

HELLEBORE

By noon, twenty-eight guests had arrived at Nachtnebel's mansion. Most were middle-aged progressives with a non-theistic view of the world. Although all were millionaires, the majority felt they were victims. It was the victim mentality. They were rebelling against life-long perceived slights and oppressions. All were advocates for social reforms. Although millionaires themselves, they believed that only they were capable of ruling the unwashed masses. They had no time for debates or discussions. Most believed in a one-world government, where elites such as themselves would rule. Many were proponents of Chaos Theory. But they all had one thing in common. They were all narcissists.

Most of Nachtnebel's staff were accepting of his idiosyncrasies, as long as they were getting paid. They chalked up his aberrant behaviors as the eccentricities of a rich old man who simply had too much time on his hands.

Time was something Nachtnebel might soon have a great deal of.

If the time machine works, thought Nachtnebel, *I could use it to go back to when I was thirty, or forty. I could use it to change everything about my life. But I've got to have the instructions. If we attempt to run it without the proper set of instructions, it could prove disastrous. Ross either has the instructions or knows how to run it from memory. Ross has to be kept alive until I get Die Glocke operating.*

Nachtnebel walked to the kitchen and checked on his staff.

"Good afternoon Mein Herr," said the Chef de Cuisine. Forty-seven-year-old Gabriel Berge had been the Chef de Cuisine, or Master Chef, for Nachtnebel for the past ten years. A graduate of the famous Ferrandi Paris culinary school, Berge got his appointment at the mansion through a referral from an actress which Nachtnebel had dated. Berge was six feet tall and weighed a toned two hundred pounds. With his short gray crew cut, Berge looked more like a stalwart sergeant major than a chef.

"How's everything coming for this evening?" asked Nachtnebel.

Berge answered, "Everything is fine, Mein Herr. We are proceeding nicely. All will be ready as you ordered."

"Very well," said Nachtnebel. "What about the hellebore?"

Hellebore is a plant which basically consists of five petal sepals surrounding a ring of nectaries. There are various species located throughout all of Europe and Asia. All hellebore plants are toxic, some extremely. Symptoms include vomiting, cramps, diarrhea, burning of the throat, depression, anaphylaxis, bradycardia, and cardiac death. There are many historical accounts of hellebore being used medicinally and nefariously throughout the ages.

In ancient times, Hippocrates (the Father of Medicine) used small doses of hellebore as a purgative. Likewise, the Greeks and Romans used it to treat gout, paralysis, and madness. It is written in Greek mythology that Dionysus cursed the daughters of King Midas with madness, and that Melampus of Pylos used hellebore to cure them. Hercules was given it after he was induced with madness by Hera and killed his children from Megara. Hellebore was also given to Alexander the Great when he took ill, and it is believed an accidental overdose may have contributed to his death.

Berge said, "Yes Mein Herr, we have enough. I have divided it into six bowls and it will be placed on the altar tonight after dinner. I will instruct your guests to only chew half of a leaf and never swallow the juice, and that they must spit out the residue, otherwise they risk becoming ill."

Nachtnebel looked at his Chef de Cuisine. "Fine, fine," he said. "We don't want anyone becoming sick. It's all just part of the fun and games. A little temptation. A little thrill. That's why they come here. What have you prepared for dinner?"

Berge said, "Mein Herr, we will start with caviar as the amuse-bouche. That will be followed by artichoke soup. The guests will then have their choice of grilled swordfish sautéed with clams, or roast prime rib of beef au jus. This will be followed by a roasted beets and goat cheese salad with walnuts, and for dessert we have prepared strawberry chocolate castle surprise."

Nachtnebel smiled.

"Sounds like you have surpassed yourself as usual Gabriel," said Nachtnebel.

Berge bowed low. "It is my pleasure Mein Herr, to always serve you."

The old billionaire turned and walked slowly out of the kitchen.

The hellebore is my Trojan Horse, thought Nachtnebel. *I'm going to use it to dispose of Ross and his friends. It is potent enough to be labeled as poison, and esoteric enough to be called accidental death. The Kantonspolizei will easily be manipulated to accept that explanation. They will have to if they want to continue receiving my monetary contributions. And as far as my guests are concerned, they will consider it thrilling to play with it, fondle it, and tease it. They are so bored with the shallowness of their empty lives that they mock death and its cold embrace.*

Nachtnebel pulled out his cellphone and called Stormbrew.

"Yes, Mein Herr," said Stormbrew.

Nachtnebel said, "Where are you now?"

"I'm with the girl, Miss Sparrow," said Stormbrew. "I've injected her with flurazepam. It's a benzodiazepine derivative. She'll be out for hours."

That's Stormbrew for you, thought Nachtnebel. *He wants to explain everything like a medical doctor, even killing.*

"Yes, yes, very well. Good work," said Nachtnebel. "How does she look to you?"

Stormbrew had Lin strapped down to a medical bed inside the room which served as a clinic to care for Nachtnebel's medical needs. Lin had been stripped of her clothes except for her bra and panties.

Stormbrew said, "She looks very beautiful, even though she is mixed racial. She appears to be half Asian."

Nachtnebel decided to tease his killer a little.

"Does that bother you, Erebus?" asked Nachtnebel.

Stormbrew replied, "No, not really. An Aryan must be willing to sacrifice for the greater good."

Nachtnebel said, "You know I'm allowing a corrider to open for Ross and his friend. I'm allowing them to use the Bergbahn to come here. The only entrance is through the hangar. They could arrive at anytime."

Stormbrew said, "Not to worry, Mein Herr. My reading of the American mentality is that Ross will not take any risks so long as Miss Sparrow is our prisoner. And then it will be too late."

Nachtnebel said with finality, "Just see that it is."

CHAPTER EIGHTEEN

NEITHER RAIN NOR SNOW

Clive Maxsted was not to be denied.

I have been a United States Department of State Foreign Service Officer for too long to allow a mere military officer to run roughshod over me! he thought.

I have negotiated with foreign officials on four continents. I have furthered US interests in 16 countries. I have engaged with local populations, worked to promote trade, and advanced democracy throughout the world.

Maxsted was patiently sitting in the Regional Polizei Office (RPO) at Am Bach 7, downtown Zermatt. He was flanked by two DSS special agents — Lee Briggs and Richard Guymon. Briggs was the more seasoned agent, having spent seven years in the Diplomatic Security Service. Guymon was new to the DSS, but was a prior military police NCO in the US Army.

The Zoom call had just started.

The polizei officer assisting with the call, Lieutenant Frederick March, was annoyed.

I've got better things to do than babysit these Americans, he thought. *Especially with one of our most prominent citizens — and most gracious contributors.*

"Good afternoon Herr Nachtnebel," said Lieutenant March to the image of the billionaire which appeared over the 75" Sony screen.

Nachtnebel replied, "Good afternoon Lieutenant."

March nodded his head and said, "I'm here with Mister Clive Maxsted from the US State Department, and Special Agents Guymon and Briggs. Mister Maxsted is one of their Foreign Service Officers."

Nachtnebel looked over the images of the men very critically.

"And how may I help you today?" Nachtnebel asked.

March said, "Well Mein Herr, it seems there is an issue with another American."

Nachtnebel immediately interrupted. "What other American?"

Maxsted seized the opportunity to jump in and take over the conversation.

"Good afternoon sir, I'm FSO Clive Maxsted. We're looking for an American soldier who may be in this area. We think perhaps he may have contacted you," said Maxsted.

Lieutenant March was furious. But he calmed himself down by slowly breathing in and out three times.

March thought to himself, *This is my country sir, and whether you work here or are visiting, you are still a foreigner, and I could still throw you and your people out, diplomatic immunity or not.*

Nachtnebel politely said, "What American soldier?"

Maxsted now had command of the conversation.

"His name is Ross, James Ross," said Maxsted.

Briggs and Guymon looked at each other and frowned.

Guymon thought, *This is plain stupid. This guy Maxsted is out of control. He's letting his personal hatred for Ross cloud the issue.*

Maxsted said, "We are inquiring if James Ross has contacted you, or attempted to contact you."

Nachtnebel said, "Gentlemen, I see many individuals every day. Mainly it is about business ventures. Is this Mister Ross perhaps in a business which I should know about?"

Maxsted decided to lay all his cards on the table.

"We feel that he may be trying to sell an antique piece of World War Two equipment," said Maxsted.

Briggs just about lost control.

Maxsted is way out of line here, Briggs thought. *I know he's my superior, but this is crazy. He's just making things up about Ross now!* But all Briggs could do was grip the arms of his chair tighter.

Nachtnebel played his role to the hilt.

"Let me see," said Nachtnebel, "I do remember a young man coming here last week …"

Maxsted leaned forward in his chair and was almost salivating.

"… but that young man was trying to sell me a 1939 Porsche Type 64 sports car. Would that be the same young man you are referring to?"

Lieutenant March looked at Maxsted hoping against hope that this could in fact be James Ross. But he knew better after he saw Maxsted's facial expression.

Maxsted appeared deflated.

"Probably not, sir," said Maxsted.

Nachtnebel smiled back.

Maxsted said, "Can you think of anyone else who may have recently contacted you about selling an antique piece of World War Two equipment, sir?"

Nachtnebel said, "Mister Maxsted, I buy and sell antiques weekly. I am what you might call — a collector. I collect vintage items from around the world. It would be easier if you could perhaps just tell me exactly what kind of equipment they were looking to sell."

Maxsted thought for a moment. Then he came up with an idea.

"We're looking for," said Maxsted, "a piece of World War Two equipment, in particular a piece of German equipment, approximately six feet wide and seven feet tall."

Nachtnebel said, "Go on."

Maxsted said, "It's a dark metallic gray color. It has electronic cables crisscrossing at its bottom and up to its top. And around the top are a bunch of little reflecting mirrors."

Nachtnebel said, "Interesting. Very interesting. But what does it look like?"

Maxsted glanced nervously at Special Agents Briggs and Guymon. Then he said, "It's about the size of a small car standing on end."

Nachtnebel pressed further. "So, it looks like an automobile? Which one?"

Maxsted replied, "Well, it ah, actually looks like a bell. A very large bell."

Nachtnebel said, "A bell? That's curious. And who made it?"

Even Lieutenant March appeared interested now.

Maxsted said, "The Germany military."

"Very curious indeed," said Nachtnebel. "I don't believe I have come across such a machine before. And what was it used for?"

Maxsted realized he had to tread lightly now. He wasn't sure if he should admit to Ansgar Nachtnebel that the Bell, Die Glocke, was in fact thought to be a Nazi time machine.

If I tell him the truth, will it make him want to obtain it even more? thought Maxsted.

"Ah, we believe it was an electrical device developed as a sort of super conductor, possibly to power turbine engines," said Maxsted.

Nachtnebel decided to jab a little.

"Oh," said Nachtnebel. "For a minute I thought you were going to tell me it was a time machine."

Maxsted sat in stunned silence. His brain scrambled for what to say next.

"There has been a sort of legend, a myth really, that began circulating about this particular machine for the past twenty-five years or so," said Maxsted. "In some esoteric occult circles, some conspiracy theorists have mentioned such a supposition."

Nachtnebel decided to poke a little bit more.

"Really?" said Nachtnebel. "And what do they give as the basis for that speculation? Do these theorists have any concrete proof?"

Maxsted realized that now this billionaire had him explaining why Die Glocke might in fact be a time machine.

Maxsted said, "Sir, it's just a myth, a fairy tale, a made-up story. It has no basis in fact. There are no such things as time machines."

Nachtnebel said, "Mister Maxsted, you are a young man. I am an old man. I don't want to take away from any experiences you may have had, but I have seen things in this world which defy your senses, defy your imagination."

Maxsted said, "Sir ..."

But Nachtnebel cut him off.

"Mister Maxsted," said Nachtnebel, "I have run across many legends in my quest for the acquisition of rare antiquities."

Maxsted said, "Yes sir, but ..."

"And, Mister Maxsted, in many instances, the legend is in fact the truth," said Nachtnebel. "The legend is whispered about in hushed tones by people who have seen the myths, lived the tale."

Maxsted tried to continue by saying, "Yes sir, and if you will permit me ..."

Nachtnebel said, "I've heard the whispers of a machine produced by the Third Reich during the war."

Maxsted looked exasperated and glanced nervously at Briggs and Guymon. The two special agents sat in their chairs implacably stoic, and unyieldingly silent.

Lieutenant March smiled and reflected to himself, *Incredible how such a simple conversation can be turned around into total chaos.* He glanced at his Doxa Sub 300 chronograph on his left wrist to note the time.

1500 hours.

Time to be wrapping this Zoom call up, thought Lieutenant March. *Time to be getting back to my policing duties.*

Maxsted tried one final time to control the narrative.

"Sir," said Maxsted, "if I may …"

Yet Nachtnebel cut him off again.

"Through my dealings in the world of collecting rare antiquities, I've heard rumors about such a machine," said Nachtnebel. "They call it Die Glocke. It would be a very exotic piece to collect indeed."

"Yes sir," said Maxsted, "and has a soldier named James Ross tried to sell you such a piece lately?"

Nachtnebel said, "Absolutely not."

CHAPTER NINETEEN

PREPARATIONS

Ross pressed the stainless steel button on the wall for Nachtnebel's Bergbahn. He and Longinus sat on a side bench adjacent to the walkway and waited patiently. In seven minutes the tram arrived.

Ross and Longinus stood up as the subway cars whizzed in front of them.

The tram came to a slow stop and its electric doors hissed open.

Ross stepped in first, followed by Longinus. Ross scanned up and down the insides of the underground train. Its seats were completely empty.

"No one at all," said Ross.

Longinus said, "As you said, Nachtnebel's inviting you."

Once they were seated, the electric doors hissed shut and the train sped away, only this time in the opposite direction.

Both men took the opportunity to check their armament while they were waiting to arrive. Longinus took out the Walther P-38 pistol and verified that the magazine was loaded with eight rounds of 9mm. Then he chambered a round. Ross did the same thing with his Beretta.

"They'll be waiting for us," said Ross. "Nachtnebel invited us. They know we're coming."

Longinus said, "Yes. How shall we play it then?"

"Nachtnebel thinks he's holding all the cards," said Ross. "He has Die Glocke, and he has Lin. But he doesn't have everything."

Longinus said, "What do you mean?"

"Remember the instruction sheets to Die Glocke?" said Ross.

Longinus nodded his head.

"I flushed them down a toilet inside the ladies' room at the Devil's Corner," said Ross. "The only instructions are here." Ross tapped his head with his index finger.

Longinus smiled and said, "Ah, the bargaining chip."

"Exactly," said Ross. "Without the instructions, Nachtnebel runs the risk of the machine malfunctioning, or even worse, disabling."

Nachtnebel's Bergbahn tunnel cut through the mountain and led down to his property. It transported passengers to arrive right outside of his huge hangar.

The side doors of the Bergbahn slid open. Ross and Longinus were hit by a blast of frigid coldness as they exited the tram. Waiting for them was Aemilius Urs, Nachtnebel's most trusted manservant.

"Welcome and good evening, gentlemen," said Aemilius.

Aemilius was opulently dressed this evening in a black tailcoat for the upcoming formal events.

Longinus and Ross looked at each other.

"My name is Aemilius Urs. Please follow me."

Ross nodded and said, "Thank you."

Aemilius turned around and led the men from the Bergbahn to Nachtnebel's massive hangar. As he approached the entrance, Aemilius took a remote control out of his pocket and pressed a button. A stainless steel double door slid open in front of them, and Aemilius led the men into the bowels of the hangar. Once they walked inside, the double doors slid shut. A blast of warmth hit them. The hangar was kept constantly heated to 73 degrees. It was a blessed relief from the bitterly cold conditions outside.

Ross and Longinus followed Aemilius through the middle of the hangar. Ross looked at the rows of vintage cars and airplanes. It reminded him of visiting the Smithsonian as a child. Then he saw Die Glocke. "Interesting stuff," said Ross, and he pointed to Die Glocke.

Longinus nodded. "Yes, interesting," he said.

Aemilius said, "I shall take you to your rooms, gentlemen. Dinner will be served at six o'clock. I will send a servant to escort you, say around thirty minutes before time. Will that be agreeable?"

Ross looked at Longinus.

"Yes," said Ross, "perfectly agreeable."

Aemilius said, "Excellent gentlemen. Of course you'll want to freshen up first. You'll each find new clothes in your closets. We only got your sizes just a few moments ago. Mister Nachtnebel prides himself on taking the utmost care of his guests."

Ross said, "That's very kind of him. And where is our host now?"

Aemilius said, "I believe he himself is resting for this evening, sir."

Longinus asked, "How many guests do you think there will be at dinner?"

Aemilius said, "Well, let me see. I do believe the number should be just over thirty, sir."

Aemilius led them to a bank of elevators on the far side of the hangar. He pressed a button and the elevator doors slid open.

"Please," said Aemilius as he motioned with his hand for Ross and Longinus to enter.

Inside the elevator, Aemilius pressed the button for the third floor.

Ross noticed the music playing inside the elevator. It was Claude Debussy's *Clair de Lune.*

In a few seconds the elevator came to a stop and the twin doors opened. Aemilius said, "Here we are, gentlemen."

Aemilius led them down the blood-red carpeted hallway which was flanked by rooms on each side. Amber Morrissey Victorian floral wallpaper lined the walls, with French Marseille Art Deco frosted crystal chandeliers hung from the ceiling every thirty feet or so.

Aemilius stopped in front of room number thirty-three.

"Here you are sir," said Aemilius as he handed an old-fashioned brass skeleton key to Ross. "This is your room, sir. And Mister Inus, your room is right across the hall, number thirty-two."

Ross took the key and said, "Thank you."

Aemilius handed the other key to Longinus, who took it without saying a word.

"One other thing sir. Every one of Herr Nachtnebel's guests will go through a metal detector before dinner," said Aemilius. "But I'm sure you are already familiar with your host's penchant for things of this nature. Will there be anything else I can do for you gentlemen?" said Aemilius.

Ross asked, "What time is it?"

Aemilius extracted a vintage Waltham pocket watch out of his vest and pushed the button to pop open the case front.

"Sir," said Aemilius, "I have approximately four-thirty-four."

Ross said, "Thank you. That'll be all."

With that, Aemilius bowed and walked back to the elevators.

Ross hefted the brass key in his hand.

"Let's talk for a minute," said Ross. Then he opened his door and Longinus followed him into the room.

The room was made up in an early 1900s Victorian style. Today you might say it was Steampunk. The entire room was wallpapered with more of the same amber Morrissey Victorian floral arrangement. There was a floral sprawl designed Toscano Victorian twin sofa next to a mahogany coffee table. The coffee table was glass inlaid with intricately carved ivory elephants. There were four chairs strategically placed throughout, with an over abundance of wall mirrors. The large floor carpet was Monarch Fire by Alexander McQueen, and it covered three-quarters of a solid oak floor. The other furniture was mostly mahogany, including the bed, which was a Jonathan Charles Versailles King, complete with four posts and hanging red canopies. The ceiling above the bed was mirrored. Ross and Longinus took in the mink-lined prison.

Ross whispered, "These rooms are more of Nachtnebel's perversions. I'm sure they're filming us right now. Let's sit and come up with a plan about what we're going to do tonight."

"Okay," whispered Longinus, and he plopped down in one of the chairs.

Ross spotted a large wooden antique Philco radio standing next to the sofa. He twisted the on/off knob to the left and turned up the volume. Classical music filled the room.

"We can't be armed at dinner, that's for sure," said Longinus.

Ross said, "Yeah. Not with every guest going through a metal detector before dinner. Looks like we're leaving our weapons here."

"Yes," said Longinus.

"But probably Nachtnebel's men will be armed. We'll just have to relieve them of their weapons after we subdue them. We must rescue Lin. That's the priority," said Ross.

Longinus new Ross was extremely efficient in planning a rescue strategy. He was in his element.

Ross said, "It appears to me there are two ways to escape from here. One way is by using Die Glocke. The other way is by flying one of Nachtnebel's aircraft out of the hangar."

Longinus said, "And you know how to operate Die Glocke."

"Yeah," said Ross. Then he looked at Longinus with a raised eyebrow. "Can you fly a plane?"

Longinus nodded his head. "As a matter of fact, yes. Yes I can fly a plane. In particular, I can fly the 190, the 229, and the Boeing."

Ross asked, "How long have you been a pilot?"

Longinus thought about the question. He was sure Ross and Lin knew who he really was. Although it was amusing to carry on this little charade, it really was unnecessary. At least it was unnecessary with Ross and Lin. And this was no time to bring up to Ross that Longinus had been a soldier in many armies over the last two thousand years, especially in the German Luftwaffe.

"I learned several years ago," said Longinus. And he left it at that.
Ross nodded.

"So," said Ross, "we have to play Nachtnebel's game tonight.
Dinner, and whatever else comes after that."

Longinus said, "If we could just somehow isolate Nachtnebel from
his guests."

"Good idea," said Ross. "Maybe we can ask him for a cocktail
after dinner. Perhaps a brandy and a cigar."

Longinus said, "He's still bound to be surrounded by his guards."

"But if we can lull him into a false sense of security, let him
believe he's holding all the cards, and then strike his guards
mercilessly," said Ross.

Longinus said, "Yes. That might just work."

Ross said, "And we already know where Die Glocke and the
planes are. The only issue is where are they holding Lin?"

Longinus nodded his head.

Ross said, "We know she'll be part of the black mass tonight. And
if all we understand about that is accurate, it should take place around
midnight. So, dinner will probably last a couple hours. And if we can
get Nachtnebel to talk to us afterwards, that will buy us the time
needed.   We know Lin will be kept alive at least until after the
ceremony. The real problem is that we need to stay alive until we can
pinpoint where Lin is being held. And for that we'll need to finesse
the information out of Nachtnebel."

Longinus asked, "And if we can't finesse him?"

Ross's face became solemn like a grave.

"I guarantee you that we will," said Ross.

Longinus looked at Ross's face.

"I believe you," he said.

Stormbrew and Nachtnebel were in the library drinking coffee in front of the well-lit fireplace.

"My dear Erebus, would you care for another cup of coffee?" asked Nachtnebel.

Stormbrew said, "Yes. I'll get it." And he picked up the pot and poured himself another cup. "No more brandy for now," said Stormbrew. "I must remain sharp for this evening."

Nachtnebel smiled. "But of course. Is Lin Sparrow still resting?"

"Yes," said Stormbrew. "We injected her with flurazepam. It's a benzodiazepine derivative. She received enough that she'll be out for a few more hours."

Nachtnebel said, "Tell me Erebus, where do you see yourself in ten years?"

Stormbrew picked up a piece of strudel and popped it into his mouth. He chewed it for a few seconds then washed the remnants down with coffee.

"You mean when I'm fifty-two? Oh I don't know. Probably I'll still be working somewhat. You know, a little bit here, a little bit there," said Stormbrew.

Nachtnebel asked, "And what about family? Do you have your own family, your own children?"

Stormbrew said, "I used to. I was married twice before. Divorced now. I have three adult children who have disowned me."

Nachtnebel said, "Oh, I'm sorry to hear that."

Stormbrew said, "It's all for the best. I enjoy my work too much."

Nachtnebel stared into the crackling fire. "I heard you mention the word *Aryan* a while back. Do you believe in the Aryan myth?"

"I'm not sure what you mean by that," answered Stormbrew.

Nachtnebel said, "The Aryan myth is a concept asserting that European people are superior to others. Hitler, Himmler, and Goebbels came up with the definition during the war."

"Yeah," said Stormbrew, "I've heard the stories. The problem with Hitler is that he didn't go far enough."

"Explain," said Nachtnebel.

Stormbrew said, "Well for one thing, he should never have declared war on the United States until he was finished building an atomic weapon. That was foolish. He should have waited. Also, Hermann Göring was developing a long-range bomber to attack New York City. Both the long-range bomber and the atomic bomb would have been game changers. The war could have been won. At least a peace accord could have been reached. Germany would probably have kept most of Europe, and Russia would never have been the superpower it is today."

Nachtnebel nodded his head up and down. "Yes, yes, quite possibly true. Would you care to hear how it really was working for the Third Reich?"

Stormbrew sat up in his chair. "Yes, I would very much."

Nachtnebel clasped both hands around his coffee cup and gazed into the fire. His face took on a faraway look. "It was as if we ruled the world," he said, "because we did in fact rule the world. It was the most extraordinary feeling."

Stormbrew said, "That feeling must have been powerful."

"Yes," said Nachtnebel. "Powerful, and yet quite overwhelming. Intoxicating it was. People were afraid of us. Nations respected us. The future was ours."

Stormbrew said, "It's hard to believe it all ended eighty years ago."

Nachtnebel picked up his cane and thumped it on the floor three times.

"Nothing ended," said Nachtnebel. "Do you see Germany today? Do you see the electric companies? They produce pure energy. Do you see the hydroelectric plants? They pump out energy. Do you see our auto manufacturers and airlines industry? This is power. This is superiority. This is national pride. Many former Nazis fled to the Swiss border. Look at our stock market. I learned a long time ago that money is power. Money is the purest form of power. With enough money, you can do anything. With enough money, you can buy anyone. With enough money, you can change the world."

Stormbrew said, "Very true, Herr Nachtnebel."

Nachtnebel looked at Stormbrew and said, "Here, let me show you something." Then he stood up and slowly shuffled towards his special display case. Stormbrew followed him. Nachtnebel carefully lifted the glass cover and tenderly picked up the watch. He handed it to Stormbrew.

Stormbrew looked at the watch and said, "This is the special watch, huh? The Benrus that Ross gave you?"

"Yes," said Nachtnebel. "He gave it to me on 20 April 1945. Turn it over. Go ahead."

Stormbrew turned the Benrus over. He read what was on the back.

"Just a bunch of names and numbers. Type I, Class A, Benrus, Department of Defense numbers, serial number, US. Oh wait a minute. I see! The manufacture date is stamped as November 2020!"

Nachtnebel smiled. "Yes. And how was an American in 1945 Berlin wearing this watch on his wrist? Simple. Because Ross and Lin Sparrow had arrived in the Die Glocke time machine. And they used the machine to then come back to the present date."

Stormbrew nodded his head.

"I plan on giving that watch back to Captain James Ross after dinner tonight," said Nachtnebel.

"And then?" asked Stormbrew.

Nachtnebel said, "After dinner, I plan on having a nightcap with Ross and his friend in the library. I want to ask them, Ross in particular, some questions. I want to know a little more about him."

"Do you need me there as well?" asked Stormbrew.

Nachtnebel shook his head. "No, I don't think so. I'll have guards with me. It will just be a little chat between old friends."

Back in his room, Ross took a quick shower and looked at the new clothes in the closet.

"Well I'll be damned," said Ross.

The clothes in the closet were almost exact duplicates of what Ross normally wore, except they were much more expensive: black Armani suit coat, black pants, white cotton Turnbull & Asser long-sleeve dress shirt, narrow black necktie, black leather shoes, and two pair of plaid boxer shorts.

And they feed the lamb before the slaughter too, thought Ross.

Ross dressed and looked at himself in the full-length mirror on the closet door.

His brown hair was hanging down across his forehead. He ran his fingers through it to push it up as best he could. Then he pocketed his wallet, cellphone, and room key. The Beretta 71 he left in the top dresser draw.

They're filming everything anyway, thought Ross. Then he opened the door and walked into the hallway, locking shut the door behind him.

He crossed the hall and knocked three times on Longinus's room.

"Come in," said Longinus.

Ross entered the room, closing the door behind him.

"How're you doing, Lon?" asked Ross.

Longinus said, "Fine. You know what? The clothes they provided me fit exactly. They seem to have had my sizes."

Longinus was dressed in a dark blue Armani suit, white Turnbull & Asser dress shirt, red necktie, and black leather shoes.

Knock.

Knock.

Knock.

Longinus looked at his 1940 Eterna chronograph wristwatch.

"Right on time," said Longinus. "The butler said he would send an escort to pick us up for dinner. Remember?"

"Yeah," said Ross.

Ross opened the door and he and Longinus looked at the escort.

"Good evening gentlemen. My name is Emma. I'm your escort for this evening."

Emma was nineteen, blonde haired, blue eyed, and beautiful. Of Scandinavian descent, Emma was wearing a black Versace Medusa 95 Crepe Midi dress, with spaghetti straps. On her feet were five inch Ellie stiletto heel pumps, with a tiny lock and key on the ankle strap.

"Are we ready?" asked Emma.

Ross and Longinus nodded.

"Very well. Follow me please," said Emma.

Emma led them down the blood-red carpeted hallway to the bank of elevators. She pressed the button and the elevator doors slid open.

Ross extended his arm and said, "After you, Emma."

Emma smiled and walked inside the elevator, closely followed by Ross and Longinus. Ross watched as she pressed the main floor button.

"The dining room is next to the library," said Emma. "I think you will enjoy dinner tonight. We're having a choice of either swordfish or prime rib."

Ross said, "That sounds delightful. So, how long have you worked for Mister Nachtnebel, Emma?"

Emma looked at Ross with curiosity.

"About seven months," she said.

Ross said, "We're here to attend the ah, party, tonight. It's our first time. Do you have any pointers to give us?"

Emma's other job was to join in with the black mass festivities by making sure the black candles were always lit, and to walk nude around both the men and women to excite them as necessary.

"Um, I would just say to enjoy yourselves and have a good time."

Then she lowered her voice and said, "Don't take it too seriously."

The elevator stopped on the main floor and the doors slid open.

"This way gentlemen," said Emma.

Ross and Longinus followed Emma as she turned a corner and led them through the metal detector, and then into the formal dining room.

Emma said, "Your host will be with you momentarily." Then Emma simply strolled away and began mingling with the thirty or so people in the room.

The formal dining room was extremely opulent. Ross estimated it to be at least 1500 square feet. The vaulted ceiling was adorned with a Sterkas crystal chandelier. The walls were of an Elizabethan style, blending late Gothic and early Renaissance influences, with gold crown molding and fluted marble pillars every twenty feet or so. Gold gilded velvet drapes covered each window. The rug was a sunburst design in red and gold, with a vibrant mythological Greek phoenix bird in the center. There was no large central dining table, but the room was peppered with smaller individual tables which could seat four patrons. In front of every plate was a placard announcing the person's name.

Ross immediately noticed the guards. There was one in each corner. Large, burly, robust men with hard faces and wearing suits. Each one was also wearing an earpiece.

They have to be armed, thought Ross. He touched Longinus on the arm and slightly nodded to one of them.

"Guards," said Ross. "One in each corner. Most probably this entire room is under surveillance."

Longinus nodded. "Yes."

Ross and Longinus slowly took in their surroundings.

Conversations of every type were taking place, from the stock market to the latest fashions. The room seemed to be buzzing with excitement. Most of Nachtnebel's guests appeared to be in their forties or fifties. There seemed to be an equal distribution of both men and women. They were well dressed, and adorned with expensive jewelry and high-end watches.

"Look," said Longinus, "here's our table."

Ross stopped walking and saw their name placards placed on one of the more central tables.

"Ladies and gentlemen," said a tuxedoed announcer at a podium. "Ladies and gentlemen may I have your attention. Please take your seats as dinner is served."

Nachtnebel's guests slowly started drifting to their tables and seats.

Ross and Longinus took their respective seats. Soon two women took the seats on either side of them.

Ross guessed the women were probably in their early forties. They were well dressed and well groomed. Both wore expensive looking necklaces.

Ross said, "Good evening. My name is James, and this is my friend Lon."

The bolder of the two women spoke up.

"My name is Ursula, and this is my partner Monique."

Then she blushed and said, "Oh I don't mean to say that we are lesbians or anything like that. I mean that Monique is actually my business partner."

Monique playfully slapped Ursula on the arm and said, "You're always embarrassing us that way!"

Ursula said, "Wait a minute. Now James, would you consider that what I said was embarrassing to anyone?"

Ross quickly looked at Longinus and then back at the women.

"Um, I don't think so," said Ross. "I certainly didn't take it that way."

Ursula playfully slapped Monique across her cheek.

"There, you see," said Ursula, "they don't think so."

Monique quickly said, "They? Who are they? I didn't hear Lon say anything?" Then she leaned forward and put her elbow on the table holding her chin in her hand and revealing her cleavage to Longinus. "What do you say, Mister Lon?"

Longinus responded quickly, "Madame, I have no earthly idea about what you are talking about."

Ursula and Monique threw their heads back and laughed outrageously.

Ursula said, "Oh you two guys are funny! You are hilarious! You are what makes these parties all the worthwhile!"

Ross smiled and said, "Yeah that's us, a barrel of monkeys."

Both women continued laughing.

Longinus sat back and thought, *Barrel of monkeys? I certainly do not understand that reference.*

The tuxedoed announcer took to the podium again.

"Ladies and gentleman if I may have your attention. I'd like to take the opportunity at this time to introduce your host for this evening, a man we all know and love, Herr Ansgar Nachtnebel."

The dining room erupted in thunderous applause.

Ross and Longinus turned their heads to view the entrance.

Ansgar Nachtnebel, with the aid of his cane, walked into the dining room. He moved fairly quickly for a ninety-one-year-old. He raised his hand and waved to his guests. The he shuffled over to the podium and picked up the microphone.

"Good evening my friends," said Nachtnebel. "I'd like to welcome you all to my humble home. This is going to be a very special evening, one you'll remember for all time." Then Nachtnebel looked at the table with Ross and Longinus. "Enjoy your dinner this evening, but leave room for dessert."

The room erupted again in thunderous applause.

Nachtnebel said, "Because this evening I have a very special treat. You all know about my sweet tooth. And tonight it will finally be satisfied."

The two women at Ross's table started giggling and clapping.

"Do you know what that means, James?" asked Ursula. "It means that tonight we will all be satiated."

Ross clenched his fist under the table.

Nachtnebel held up his hands to quiet the applause.

"Now ladies and gentlemen," said Nachtnebel, "please enjoy the evening." Then he walked away from the podium and took his seat at the table directly in front of Ross's, so he could view Ross whenever he wanted to.

Longinus leaned over to Ross and whispered, "Reminds me of the elites in Rome."

Monique saw what Longinus did and said, "Now hey you two, what are you whispering about over there? That's very naughty." And then she shook her finger. "Naughty, naughty."

Longinus said, "Madame, I can assure you I am not naughty."

Ursula and Monique just giggled.

Servants soon arrived with trays of steaming food. Ursula and Monique received the grilled swordfish. Ross and Longinus were both given the prime rib.

"Smells good," said Ross picking up his knife and fork.

Longinus bent his head in silent prayer. Ross saw him and followed suit. Monique and Ursula stopped cutting their food and watched.

Monique leaned over to Ursula and whispered, "They're praying."

"I see," whispered Ursula. "Real men at last."

The dinner moved along rapidly, and soon servants arrived to take away the plates.

The servant removing Ross's plates handed him a folded note and said, "From the host, sir."

Ross looked over at Nachtnebel and their eyes caught. Nachtnebel lifted his champagne goblet to salute Ross. Ross saw the gesture and lifted the note.

Ross slit the paper seal holding the note closed with his thumbnail. The note said to meet in the library next door after dinner for a nightcap. Then Ross gave the note to Longinus.

"Secret notes, eh?" said Ursula.

Ross smiled.

Soon the dessert arrived. Servants placed the strawberry chocolate castle surprise plates in front of them.

"Mmmm," said Monique, "I just love chocolate cake with strawberries. Don't you?"

Longinus said matter-of-factly, "Indeed, Madame."

Ross noticed Nachtnebel get up and walk away from his table towards the exit.

"Let's go," said Ross to Longinus. "Pardon me ladies but you must excuse us."

Ross and Longinus left the table and walked out of the formal dining room. The guard closest to the doors raised his arm and talked into his sleeve cuff.

"They're alerting Nachtnebel that we're on our way," said Ross.

Longinus nodded.

Ross pulled open the twelve-foot-tall mahogany double doors of the library, and he and Longinus walked in. The library was dark except for the flickering flames in the large marble fireplace. They crackled and sizzled as if in beckoning them to enter.

The library held Nachtnebel's vast collection of treasures, from Egyptian art to Mesopotamian artifacts. The walls were adorned with paintings from Picasso, Degas, and Matisse. His library walls housed first editions of Hemingway, Steinbeck, Poe, Cervantes, Dostoevsky, and Hugo.

Nachtnebel was already inside the library sitting in one of his plush red leather-bound chairs next to the grand fireplace. Two chairs were placed facing him. One was for Ross. The other was for Longinus. Between them sat a small table complete with brandy decanter, ice bucket, and three glasses.

Ross and Longinus scanned the scene.

In particular, they were looking for where any guards would be.

He's got to have guards somewhere, but I just don't see them yet, thought Ross.

"Please come in, come in gentlemen," said Nachtnebel. "Come in and sit down. Make yourselves comfortable."

Ross and Longinus each took a seat in front of Nachtnebel.

"May I offer you a drink?" asked Nachtnebel.

Ross thought, *I only want Lin and to get out of this crazy house.*

"All right," said Ross.

Nachtnebel leaned forward and poured Ross and Longinus a brandy.

"Ice?" he asked.

"Yes for me," said Ross.

Longinus said, "Yes, thank you."

Nachtnebel leaned back and said, "Have no fear gentlemen, the brandy is not drugged."

Ross still sniffed his glass nonetheless.

Nachtnebel said, "I've asked you here before the evening's activities climax. I wanted to talk, to get to know you a little bit."

Nachtnebel stared directly into Ross's piercing dark brown eyes. "Tell me," he said, "you are the man who saved me all those years ago, aren't you?"

Ross knew the moment had come. He looked at Longinus his friend, and then back at Nachtnebel his enemy.

"Yes," said Ross, "yes I am."

Nachtnebel smiled and thumped his fist on the arm of his chair.

"I knew it. I just knew it," said Nachtnebel. "I've waited all of these years for this moment. I knew it from the watch you gave me."

Ross looked puzzled.

Nachtnebel said, "The Benrus, remember? You gave me your watch back in 1945."

Ross said, "I remember."

Nachtnebel put his drink down and stood up. "Let me show you something." He walked directly to the display case and lifted the glass.

Longinus watched Nachtnebel return to his seat and hand Ross an object.

"This is the Benrus you gave me all those years ago. Take a look at the caseback," said Nachtnebel.

Ross turned his watch over and looked at the stampings. Then he saw it.

"Yes," said Nachtnebel. "You see, don't you? The manufacturer's date? It's stamped on the caseback."

Ross said, "November 2020."

Nachtnebel thumped his fist again on the arm of his chair.

"Exactly!" exclaimed Nachtnebel. "And there is only one way a man as young as you could have given me that watch way back in 1945. The only way is by using the Nazi time machine Die Glocke!"

Ross looked at his Benrus. The time was already set and the watch appeared to be operating normally. He strapped it to his left wrist.

"Let's get down to business," said Ross. "We're here for Lin Sparrow. Where is she?"

Nachtnebel said, "She's here somewhere. She's going to be a vital part in our revelry this evening."

"But why?" asked Ross. "Why Lin? I saved your life."

Nachtnebel said, "Yes, you did indeed save my life. It was 1945 and I was eleven years old. A time of war. I surely would have been killed by the Russians. You did indeed save my life."

Longinus was thinking, *Enough of this. Let's kill this man and find Lin.*

Nachtnebel asked, "Do you remember a man named Doctor Wu Qiang?"

Ross said, "Yes."

"I'm sure you do," said Nachtnebel. "He was my very good friend. You killed him. You also destroyed my plans to acquire the Spear of Destiny, and you killed multiple Chinese agents in the process."

Longinus spoke up. "James didn't kill Wu Qiang. I did."

Nachtnebel shifted his gaze to Longinus for the first time.

"What?" said Nachtnebel.

"That's right," said Longinus, "and as far as the spear goes, you have no earthly idea of the unspeakable powers you are meddling with."

Nachtnebel was stunned.

"Who exactly are you, sir?" asked Nachtnebel.

Ross looked at Longinus and nodded once.

Longinus stood up and said, "I am Longinus — Centurian to the Legionnaires of Rome — husband to a long dead wife — father to three long dead children — crucifier of the Son of Man — beholder of the miracle at Golgotha — and I demand you release Lin Sparrow now!"

Ross and Longinus sprang forward and pounced on Nachtnebel.

The chair Nachtnebel was sitting in tumbled backwards, and with the combined weight of Ross and Longinus, splintered into pieces. The ninety-one-year-old Nachtnebel frantically clutched his chest and lost consciousness.

Four guards armed with Heckler & Koch MP5K 9mm submachine guns rushed into the room.

RAT-A-TAT-TAT!

RAT-A-TAT-TAT!

RAT-A-TAT-TAT!

Hot lead was blazing by Ross and Longinus like so many angry wasps. Bullets splintered the furniture and embedded into the walls and floor.

Ross and Longinus immediately charged the guards and tackled them. A furious hand-to-hand melee commenced. Ross lashed out punching guards and trying to control their weapons. It was a feverish combative free for all. Longinus grabbed a guard's MP5K and shoved the barrel up and under his chin, pulling the trigger and blasting the man's skull to pieces. Blood splashed across Longinus's face, while he violently smashed his elbow into another guard's solar plexus and then smashed his palm up and into the nose, sending shards of jagged bone into the man's brain. Ross grabbed a guard by his jaw and temple and violently twisted the man's head, hideously snapping his neck. The guard's lifeless body crumpled to the ground like a rag doll. More bullets whizzed by Ross's head, but he quickly leg-swept the guard and followed him to the floor with both hands on the guard's throat. Ross quickly reached up and pressed both his thumbs into the man's eye sockets blinding him.

"Eeeeeowwww!" gruesomely screamed the guard.

Longinus stood over him with an MP5K and shot the guard once through the forehead.

Ross wiped his hands with the bloody muck down his pants leg, and picked up from the floor a Heckler & Koch MP5K 9mm submachine gun.

"Let's get the hell outta here," said Ross.

They hurried to the twelve-foot-tall mahogany double doors of the library. Ross slung his weapon for a second and grabbed the door handles, then he threw open the doors.

Outside the scene was total utter chaos. Nachtnebel's guests were screaming and running helter-skelter in the hallway. An overhead alarm siren started blaring:

ARUU-GAA!

ARUU-GAA!

ARUU-GAA!

"We've got to find Lin!" yelled Ross. Then he saw Emma running down the hall. Ross grabbed her quickly by the arm almost pulling it out of the socket.

"Where's Lin Sparrow?" demanded Ross.

Emma looked at Ross like he was crazy.

"Who?" said Emma.

Ross repeated, "Where's Lin Sparrow?"

Emma squirmed in his vice-like grip.

"I don't know anyone named that!" Emma cried.

Ross yelled, "Where's the girl sacrifice? Where's the girl who is to be sacrificed?"

Emma said, "In the black mass chapel."

"Where is that?" yelled Ross.

Emma pointed with her finger. "Four rooms down on the left."

Ross released his grip on her arm and he and Longinus sprinted down the hall. They soon saw the chapel and knew it was for the black mass by a four foot black cross hung upside down on its doors.

"This is it!" yelled Longinus over the blasting noise of the alarm.

Ross tried the doorknobs, but the doors where locked.

He stepped back, leveled his MP5K, and blasted the door locks to pieces. Then Ross kicked open the doors.

"Jesus Christ," said Ross.

The scene inside the black mass chapel was reminiscent of something straight out of Dante's Inferno or the Spanish Inquisition. The entire chapel was dark, except at intervals illuminated by the flickering flames of thick six-foot-tall black candles. There were two sets of ten wooden pews running parallel with each other straight up to an altar. Instead of having the traditional Stations of the Cross markers on the walls, there hung instead the most obscene alabaster pornographic carvings of gang rape scenes, BDSM scenes, sexual torture scenes, and multiple busts of Lucifer himself. In front of the altar was a huge six-foot-tall X cross. Not a traditional crucifixion cross, but one on its side to resemble a large X. Strapped to the X cross and spread-eagled was Lin Sparrow. Lin was stripped nude with bowls of leafy hellebore plants and dozens of black roses on either side of her. She was gagged and struggling against her bonds. There were several red welts across her abdomen. A man stood in front of Lin holding a black leather flogger. The man was naked and fully aroused.

In the middle of the man's chest was tattooed a Swastika.

"Stormbrew!" yelled Ross.

Erebus Stormbrew dropped his flogger and turned around.

"Captain Ross," said Stormbrew. "I should have killed you back in Zurich when I had the chance."

Outside the chapel, three of Nachtnebel's armed guards rushed the doors. Longinus swung around and took a knee, firing his weapon at the guards.

"I got this!" yelled Longinus.

Ross was seething with rage and dropped his MP5K. It clattered to the ground. Then he charged Stormbrew.

Stormbrew threw a series of Korean Taekwondo arm strikes and leg kicks at Ross, but Ross countered by blocking most of them successfully.

Ross spun and performed a roundhouse kick to Stormbrew's jaw which caught him by surprise.

Stormbrew spat out blood and said, "I see you've had some training, Green Beret."

Ross lashed out with a solid right-handed punch to Stormbrew's face. The nose crunched under his knuckles and fresh blood splattered across Stormbrew's face. He fell backwards over one of the legs of the X cross.

Stormbrew reached behind the X cross for something. When he stood up, he had in his hands a Japanese katana sword.

"Ross," gasped Stormbrew, "you won't disrupt my purification of this timeless goddess."

Ross could see Lin struggling against her bonds.

Ross yelled, "What the hell is wrong with you man? It's over. You can't win!"

Stormbrew said, "Oh but we can Captain Ross, and we will. Nothing can stop the Aryan Disciples of Lucifer."

CHAPTER TWENTY

TIMELESS GODDESS

A katana is a single-edged sword that has a curved blade. The golden age of katana production was in the fourteenth century. The word itself in Japanese — katana — means *one-sided blade*.

Stormbrew held the Japanese katana sword professionally, with two hands. The right hand placed above the left.

Stormbrew's eyes met Ross's for a second, and then Stormbrew lashed out with a deadly forward thrust of the sword. Ross quickly sidestepped the blade and locked his forearms around Stormbrew's neck in a chokehold. Stormbrew altered his hold of the katana to only his right hand. He brought the sword up in a wild swipe backwards towards Ross's head. Ross ducked and increased the pressure on Stormbrew's neck with his chokehold.

"Arrggh," moaned Stormbrew.

Ross leaned slightly back and continued applying maximum pressure and his entire body weight to Stormbrew's neck.

Stormbrew dropped the sword and began to grow limp.

Ross's choke technique would result in constriction of air flow to the lungs and blood flow to the brain. But Ross was not interested in merely seeing Stormbrew pass out.

Crack!

That was the sound Ross was waiting for. The beautiful sound of Stormbrew's neck breaking.

Ross released his grip and allowed Stormbrew's body to fall to the floor.

Longinus had killed three of the guards with his automatic weapons fire, and now the fourth guard turned and retreated down the hallway.

Longinus stood up and turned around. He saw Stormbrew's naked grotesque dead body, and Ross standing in front of Lin removing her mouth gag.

"Oh my God, James!" blurted out Lin. "What an insane asylum this place is!"

Ross untied the leather straps binding Lin's wrists and feet to the X cross. Then he took off his suit coat and tenderly wrapped it around her.

"Here," said Ross. "Are you badly hurt?"

Lin shook her head. "No, not really," she said. "Let's just get out of this place."

The overhead alarm siren suddenly stopped. Ross picked up his MP5K and looked at Longinus.

"We've got to get to the hangar," said Ross. "It's the only way outta here."

Longinus flicked his selector switch to semi to conserve ammo.

"Right," said Longinus. "You take care of Lin. I'll lead. This way," said Longinus motioning with his thumb.

Lin buttoned up the suit coat and held Ross's hand for dear life. In Ross's other hand he held the Heckler & Koch MP5K 9mm submachine gun at the ready.

The scene outside the black mass chapel was eerily silent. The alarm had stopped blaring, and the hallways seemed to be empty of everyone.

What's going on? thought Ross.

Nachtnebel's guests had considered the evening's activity much too violent, and most were in their rooms packing their belongings and heading out to the Bergbahn.

Longinus skillfully moved down the hallway, checking around every corner for guards. Ross closely followed with Lin. They came to a bank of elevators. Ross pressed the down button.

Ross said, "I remember in the elevator today with Aemilius that there was a button for the hangar."

The elevator doors slid open, and the three friends stepped inside.

Longinus scanned the control panel.

"Here it is," said Longinus, and he pressed the yellow button labeled *HANGAR*.

The elevator doors automatically closed and they started to descend.

Inside the elevator, Longinus said, "I think you and Lin should take Die Glocke."

"And what about you?" asked Ross.

Longinus said, "I'm going to fly out with the Pan Am Clipper."

"The Clipper?" said Ross. "But it doesn't even have landing gear."

"That's true," said Longinus. "It has what we pilots call sponson stabilizing floats built over the fuselage. It's on a trailer inside the hangar attached to a tractor. All I need is for you to drive the tractor and pull me out into the snow. Then I can slide down the mountain with the engines running until I achieve escape velocity."

Ross thought for a second. "On any other night that might sound strange, but not tonight," said Ross. "So where will you land it?"

"Ah, that's the beautiful part — in the Danube. That river runs right through Vienna. I'll land it on the water and simply leave the plane. Then I'll walk to my apartment."

"Okay Lon, that sounds like a plan," said Ross. "Then I'll run back to Die Glocke and transport Lin and I outta here."

The elevator doors slid open and they were inside the hangar. All still seemed quite normal, and the only abnormality was upstairs with the guests scrambling to gather their belongings and get on the Bergbahn.

Thank God the temperature inside this hangar is regulated, thought Ross. Otherwise Lin, who was naked except for Ross's suit coat jacket, would be freezing.

"Let me get Lin inside Die Glocke first," said Ross.

Longinus nodded and said, "I'll go open the hangar doors."

Lin held Ross's hand and they ran to Die Glocke.

Ross spun the circular nautical hatch handle counterclockwise on Die Glocke and tugged on it. The hatch opened and Ross peered inside. *Everything looks normal,* he thought.

He held Lin's hand and helped her step inside. Lin sat down in the Luftwaffe pilot's seat and said, "I'm all right. You guys go."

Ross said, "Power up the machine while I'm gone."

Longinus raised the hangar doors and then ran back to Die Glocke. He poked his head inside the machine and said, "Lin, may God always bless you, and may Heaven's stars shine upon you."

Lin reached out and touched Longinus's hand. "God bless you Lon," said Lin. "Take care of yourself, and thank you."

Ross unslung his MP5K and handed it to Lin.

"Here," said Ross. "Hang on to this. I'll be right back."

Then Ross closed the hatch but didn't lock it.

Ross turned to Longinus and said, "Let's go."

The friends ran to the Boeing Pan Am 314 Clipper aircraft. Longinus grabbed the handle of the entry hatch and twisted it counterclockwise. The hatch opened and Longinus scrambled inside. Ross was busy unbuckling cargo straps which were securing the plane to the trailer.

I hope this thing doesn't slide off too soon, thought Ross.

Then Ross ran to the front of the trailer and climbed into the attached tractor. Ross saw that the keys were already in the ignition.

Thank God, thought Ross.

He activated the choke, turned the ignition key to the right, and the tractor engine sputtered to life. Ross turned around in the seat to see how Longinus was doing.

Longinus sat in the cockpit and looked like a mad scientist behind all the blinking dashboard lights. He checked the fuel level, brakes, adjusted the flaps, and lastly strapped himself in with the seat harness.

Longinus glanced out each side window at the engines. Then he pressed the starter button.   The four Wright GR2600A2 engines choked, then sputtered, then roared to life with grayish-blue smoke billowing out of their exhausts.

"Hmm," mused Longinus. *Probably have worn piston rings,* he thought. *No time to fret about that now.*

Longinus gave Ross the thumbs-up symbol through the cockpit windscreen. Ross saw the thumbs-up and returned the gesture.

All right let's go, thought Ross. He put the tractor in gear and pressed the accelerator pedal.   The trailer with the huge Pan Am Clipper started moving forward.

Ross was pleased. *So far so good,* thought Ross.

The tractor had no trouble whatsoever towing the trailer with the aircraft.

Ross steered towards the hangar entrance. He only turned around once to look back at the Clipper. It was still on the trailer.

No sweat, thought Ross.

Then they were through the hangar entrance and the cold mountain winds buffeted them mercilessly. Ross continued driving forward until he was sure the entire trailer was through the entrance. He began to notice the terrain gradually sloping down the mountainside. Then he put the tractor in park and climbed down from the seat. He went to the rear and disengaged the tow hitch. Ross waved to Longinus signaling that everything was all right. He climbed back onto the tractor and drove around to the rear of the trailer.   Then Ross slowly put the tractor in low gear and proceeded to push the trailer forward down the slope.

Inside the cockpit, Longinus was revving the engines. The trailer started to pick up speed as the slope down the mountain increased.

The trailer started to outrun the tractor down the mountainside. Ross applied the brakes and turned the tractor around. He looked one more time at his friend and then put the tractor in gear and headed back to the hangar.

Longinus was ready. Every fiber of his body was attuned to the situation. The trailer was gathering more and more speed racing down the mountain, with Longinus gunning the aircraft engines. Then he saw it.

"A boulder," said Longinus. "Directly in front and right in my path. This is it."

Longinus gunned the engines and pulled back on the yoke with all his might. The Clipper nose pitched upwards and generated the right amount of lift needed for the Boeing to steadily climb in altitude. Just then the trailer smashed into the boulder, but the Boeing had lifted off and was soaring upwards.

Ross turned around in his seat again and saw the 1938 Boeing Pan Am 314 Clipper take flight and continue to ascend.

He'll make it, thought Ross.

Ross drove the tractor through the hangar entrance and parked it beside Die Glocke.

Looks like we're going to make it, thought Ross.

BA-RAT-A-TAT-TAT!

BA-RAT-A-TAT-TAT!

BA-RAT-A-TAT-TAT!

Bullets began whizzing by Ross's head and pinging off the tractor.

Ross ducked and took cover behind the tractor. He could make out three of Nachtnebel's guards who were now in the hangar and advancing on him.

I have no weapon to return fire, thought Ross. *If I could just make it into Die Glocke!*

But the hot lead was peppering the tractor and getting closer and closer to Ross.

Goddamnit! thought Ross. *We were so close.*

The three guards must have guessed Ross had no gun, as now they stood up from behind their covered positions and advanced on Ross.

Ross poked his head up from behind the tractor, only to be met by more bullets zipping by.

BA-RAT-A-TAT-TAT!

God, prayed Ross, *Just let Lin get outta here. Let her survive.*

The three guards were now almost directly in front of Die Glocke and steadily advancing on Ross.

CLANG!

Suddenly the hatch of the Die Glocke machine sprang open and automatic weapons fire erupted from within. A hail of bullets cut down the first two guards, and then Lin Sparrow stepped out of the machine barefoot and only wearing Ross's suit coat, firing her MP5K submachine gun, and showing a bit more thigh than usual. The third guard turned and pointed his weapon at Lin, but she cut him down with a burst of automatic gunfire.

RAT-A-TAT-TAT!

The third guard crumpled to the ground next to the other two.

Lin stood her ground with the barrel of her MP5K still smoking.

Ross stood up from behind the tractor and walked over to Lin. He took the smoking submachine gun from her hands and let it fall to the ground.

"Let's go," said Ross.

Ross climbed into Die Glocke first, followed by Lin who had to sit on his lap in the Luftwaffe pilot's seat.

Lin leaned forward and pulled the hatch closed. She spun the inside circular handle clockwise until it stopped. Then she tugged at it one more time to make sure. Ross secured them both in the seat with the *fallschirmjäger,* or "paratrooper" harness.

Ross scanned the control panel searching for the *macht auf* switch, otherwise translated to "power on" button. He flipped up the plastic safety cover and pressed the button, which immediately started to glow an ancient amber luminescence. Then Ross set the trip parameters and the GPS coordinates. The grid coordinates function was a very primitive 1940s-era direction-distance-location dashboard map screen which allowed you to input latitude and longitude coordinates. Next, Ross pressed the Trolit Thermoplast button on top of the *gangschaltung* (gear shift) control lever.

Ross looked at his Benrus watch. It was midnight.

Lin snuggled against him. "And you just saved the world again, my love," she said.

"We did," replied Ross. "You have the honors. Ready?"

Lin reached forward for the lever and said, "Yes."

"Let's go," said Ross.

Lin ratcheted the control lever forward.

Clack, clack, clack.

The sounds coincided with the spinning of the control panel grid coordinates dial.

Clack, clack, clack.

If Ross and Lin could have seen the outside of Die Glocke, they would have been amazed. The base of the machine was emitting a greenish-orange glow, and the entire outer capsule was starting to vibrate. The clacking sound inside was in competition with a swirling, rushing, windstorm sound outside growing in intensity.

Soon Die Glocke became an enormous greenish-orange glowing orb, and then it simply vanished amidst a whirlwind of swirling dust and crackling static electricity.

All that remained from Die Glocke where it had stood on the concrete hangar floor was a sizzling, steaming, crystallized sheet of glass.

EPILOGUE

It is unknown the place and uncertain the time where death awaits you; thus you must expect death to find you, every time, and every place.

Lucius Annaeus Seneca
4 BC — 65 AD
Roman Stoic Philosopher

SOMEWHERE IN TIME

FSO Clive Maxsted was nervously sitting in a waiting area outside the Oval Office in Washington DC. He was there to brief the President of the United States on operation *Timeless Goddess.*

I've already briefed General Matthews at the Pentagon, he thought. *That didn't go over very well.*

Maxsted anxiously fidgeted in his seat.

It's been two weeks, and no one has heard from Ross, he thought. *The debacle at Ansgar Nachtnebel's mansion really caused panic. FBI, CIA, Interpol, Swiss FIS, and Mossad are swarming all over that place. No one seems to be talking.*

Maxsted shifted restlessly in his chair.

A female White House Intern walked briskly towards Maxsted.

"Excuse me sir, but are you Mister Maxsted?" asked the beautiful young Intern.

"Ah, yes," said Maxsted. "Yes I am."

The Intern said, "I have a package for you. Here you are." She handed the box to Maxsted.

Package for me? thought Maxsted. *What?*

Maxsted took the small box and opened it.

Inside the box, delicately wrapped in tissue paper, was a single black rose.

THE END

ABOUT THE AUTHOR

Bernard Cenney retired from the United States Army as a Lieutenant Colonel after more than twenty-eight years in uniform. He considers it a privilege to have served his country throughout numerous command and staff assignments the world over. He makes Texas his home.